Until We Meet Again

Lucas Hayes

Contents

Prologue

Before the night of August 2nd, I guess I did what you'd call take life for granted.

I take full responsibility for what happened that night. If I'd been there for her, she wouldn't have driven herself to die. She would have known just how much I cared about her. She was my best friend and all and always will be.

I guess, even after Melinda killed herself, I've still been taking life for granted. I haven't appreciated it, and have gone out, and lived. I haven't experienced life experiences a college sophomore should. In fact, I'm as close as innocent as they come. I don't even do normal life things.

I've even created a list of the things I'd never done that Melinda HAD done in high school alone.

I'd called it:

Ally's list of why she's such a loner.

1. Never smoked weed or a cigarette.

2. Never drank, or have gotten drunk.

3. Never have I ever driven a car just because.

4. Gone roller-skating.

5. Kissed anyone.

6. Had a campfire.

7. gone camping itself.

8. Gone fishing.

9. Swam in a public pool.

10. Had sex.

11. Gone hiking.

12. Jumped off a cliff.

13. Pretended to become engaged to get food.

14. Been to the zoo out of my sheer fear of anything animals.

15. Been to a party.

16. Thrown a party.

17. Had an actual birthday party.

18. Decorated anything - including my apartment.

19. Gotten a tattoo.

20. Raised anything whatsoever.

21. Gambled.

22. Fallen in love.

23. Gone shark cave diving.

24. Never out loud said the word: "fuck".

25. Gone scuba diving.

26. Seen the Eiffel Tower.

27. Water skiing.

28. Been on a rollercoaster that goes upside down.

29. Gone whitewater rafting.

30. Gone on a hot air balloon.

31. Windsurfed.

32. Been on a date.
33. Ridden a camel.
34. Ridden a motorcycle.
35. Sleep under the stars.
36. Built an igloo.
37. Go to a nightclub.
38. Gone to a Coachella show.
39. Gotten my future told.
40. Kiss a stranger.
41. Go skinny dipping.
42. Go streaking in a park.
43. Let go of my past.
44. Watch the sunset/rise.
45. Eat one of those ant-in-candy lollipops.
46. Send a message in a bottle.
47. Dance in the rain.
48. Forgive someone major in my life.
49. Make a donation.
50. Make any type of impact on a person or the world.

Those were all things I'd been around for to witness the incredible Melinda do with her life. I'd written them all down because these were things I'd never done.

Before you ask no I did not watch my best friend have sex with someone. She told me about it. In fact, she told me about most of these things.

I'd never done any of these with her, for some reason. A few I could have, but walked away from. She'd done them with the person she'd thought was her best friend, the person who in the end would be the reason her life ended.

If I'd paid more attention...

If only I'd paid more attention...

Now, I'm a girl who always wears jeans, a jacket, and Converse to school. I do my work and go to bed at the end of the day. I'm not popular, in fact, Melinda had been my only friend other than a small Japanese girl named Lynn who'd confessed her attraction towards me on the summer of senior year, our year going into college when I'd gotten my braces removed, my acne decided it was farewell, and for some reason, my breasts decided to grow one more cup larger and into a 32 C and my legs started to suit me very well.

Still.

But..

This was all about to change.

Chapter 1

It all started around late in May. My life changing that is.

I'd forever be used to not being good enough, half did I know, half did I not. My mind was set. I knew where I was going, what I'd be doing, that is until May 14th.

The day I met Parker West.

"Ally! Coffee spill, do you mind getting it for me?" My roommate asks as the doorbell rings. I nod and stand. I grab a paper towel and start cleaning the counter slowly. In comes Sam, Laney's boyfriend.

"Babe!" Laney squeals, pulling him to her in a hug. I smile down at the paper towel. Their love for each other is so visible.

"Hey L." He says. "Hey Ally." He greets. I look up, sending a small wave. I throw the paper towel out and lean against the counter, pulling out my phone and replying to my cousin.

"I can't believe Kehls and Ryder just started school." She states. They talk about these two people a lot. I have yet to meet them, but they seem okay.

"They just wanted time to spend with each other before multi-tasking. I guess every one of her new roommates did the same thing. Weird." He says. I see her nod.

"That is odd. She better not replace me." She says, and he laughs.

"One of them is her old friend, Laila." He says.

"Bitch better not square up, that's my best friend." She replies lowly. I laugh to myself as I continue texting.

"Hey Ally, when did you start college?" Sam asks me. I look up.

"As soon as high school ended. I wanted to get out of the hell hole called a small town." I tell him. He laughs, nodding, agreeing.

"Ooh. We're gonna be late. See you later, Ally!" Laney says with a smile on her face, hooking her arm with Sam's and dragging him out. He waves to me quickly before disappearing. I chuckle lowly. They're perfect for each other.

The door suddenly opens again.

"Oh and Ally, you should get out more." Laney states before shutting the door. I stare at where she was just moments before for what seems like minutes. She's right. I should.

For now, I'll stick to school.

I grab my backpack from my bedroom, throwing in random folders - I don't know which is which because I'm so obsessed with the color Mint Green that they're all the same - and shut my backpack after carefully placing my MacBook in there.

I pull it over my shoulders before walking out.

I guess it wouldn't hurt to go to Starbucks for a bit and study or something. I get there and ignore the curious looks of classmates, seeing as I've never come here before, and get a caramel ribbon crunch Frappuccino before sitting in a window seat. I open my backpack and take out my Mac. I set the backpack on the strap on the chair.

And, I guess that's how it all started for me. Placing that bag right there. I mean, it'd be the beginning of doom for Sophomore year me, but looking back at it, I'm so happy I did that.

I sit and scroll through Instagram on the computer, bored. I continue to do so.

Suddenly, the chair my backpack rests on skids, falling over because someone was pushed into it.

Not just someone.

Parker West. Well known around campus, Parker was at-tractive, a basketball player on the verge of getting signed and pulling as many bitches imaginable. Basically, one of the hottest and most popular boys at our University. He laughs it off until he realizes he just dumped my things everywhere. He leans down and starts to reach for the papers to pick them up. His eyes skim over the words, and his lips turn up. He glances at me.

"Interesting." He murmurs, handing the paper to me. It reads:

Ally's list of why she's such a loner.

I instantly feel my cheeks burn, so I get to the floor and pick up the rest of the stuff before he can see anything else that might possibly be in there.

"You're... Ally Smith, right?" He asks. I nod, and put my Mac back in my bag. "Hey, uh, you don't have to leave yet." He says. He looks morbidly shocked, probably upon actually seeing me anywhere other than the classes we have together.

"Uh, no, I finished my drink anyways." I mumble and look over to the open trash can. I pick up the cup and toss it. It makes it perfectly. I smile in satisfaction.

"Wow that was pretty impressive. Think you could take me in a game of basketball?" He asks with a slight smirk. That was his sport. Little did anyone know it was my sport too. Not that I did anything with it. I just wanted to be a reporter.

I let a small, nervous laugh. I don't talk to guys much, other than Sam or my brother, so I was admittedly very nervous.

"Uh.. Probably." I answer honestly. "Your defense is a little weak, and your shots are too tightened. You need to loosen up a bit." I tell him before realizing what I just said. "Not that you aren't good or anyth-"

He cuts me off by laughing. "No, you're fine.. Actually, thanks for the advice." He says. I smile shyly before awkwardly waving my hand with a very tiny shrug and walking away. "I'll- uh - see you in class." he calls. I glance back and shyly smile. I notice people watching the exchange. Girls sip their coffee while pursing their lips, eyes narrowing in my direction.

The next morning, I'm sitting at the counter by myself. Laney never came back, and I honestly don't want to know what her and Sam were doing last night in order for her not to come home.

I sip my coffee while reading the paper.

Suddenly, there's three quiet taps at my door. I glance down at my outfit. Jean short shorts, and a black tank top. I shrug and open the door.

There, stands Parker West. He takes in my appearance for a second. His gaze lingers on my long legs that I personally hate. I was pretty tall for a girl, something I'd always been insecure about.

"You should really show those legs off more." He mutters. His eyes raise to my face, which now has eyes looking like flying saucers. He smiles at the reaction. "Can I come in?" He asks calmly. I numbly step back and he comes in. He looks around and whistles in appreciation to the apartment. I got to admit, my apartment is pretty bomb. Its all modern, black and white furniture, marble counter tops, amazing balcony right out of the living room.

"How did you... Why are you.."

"How did I find you and why am I here?" He offers, still looking at the apartment more than me. I'm okay with that. "One, the staff. Two, I'm here about that list." He states. I instantly blush, and he looks over to me.

"Uh.. That's nothing." I mumble.

"Really? Dude, you've never even gone camping. That is sad." He states. I flinch slightly, hurt.

"Geez. Sorry I didn't do something." I state, rolling my eyes. He doesn't know. He doesn't know.

"I mean, you should do those things on there." He says. "So I'm here to help." He says, a smile growing his features.

I stay silent, confused.

Then it clicks.

"Oh, no, really n-"

"Oh yes, really yes." He says brightly. "You're always alone, you never go out, you have a sad look in your eyes. I want to get you to do those things on your list. I'm here to help. Call me godsent." he says.

"More like hell's angel." I correct him.

"At least I'll still be attractive." He says, running a hand through his hair, making it even messier if possible. I laugh once, quietly. What a lame line. "So you in or not?" He asks, holding out a hand. I stare at it. "Come on, Ally. It'll be fun. Live for once. Get out there. You only get a certain amount of time on earth, might as well use it." He says, instantly reminding me of Melinda.

Caught me at a moment of weakness.

I hold out my hand, and shake his.

"..Deal."

Chapter 2

I walked through the doors, Parker behind me, reading off random things we could do first.

He doesn't even have the list in his hand. He has photographic memory.

Of course he does. He was known for being a very multi-talented kind of guy, so why should I expect anything less?

"We could go camping tonight." He says. I glance at him, ignoring the curious/shocked expressions from the fellow nosey peers.

"Its a school night, Parker." I remind him. He snaps his fingers. I sit in my usual seat in the corner of the room, and he sits beside me.

"Hmm. Oh, I know!" He says, a smile growing over his features. "We coul-"

"Hey West! What are you doing?! Get over here, idiot!" One of his friends call out to him. He looks over. He looks back to me.

"Your one of those guys, aren't you? Yes, yes you are." I decide before even giving him a chance to reply.

"What?" He asks, his smile slowly fading.

"Your one of those guys that sit with the jocks and act like them for reputation, but you don't want it, do you? You don't care about the reputation, or the popularity. You just like the game, and with the game, comes the issue of those douchebags." I murmur quietly. His lips twitch.

"And you figured this out how?" He queries.

I lean forward slightly. "Because if you were one of them, you would look at that list, and you'd laugh at me. You'd say I have no life, and I never will have a life because guys like those ones are bullies. But here you are wanting to help me fulfill my list." I whisper. That heart-breaking, perfect smile finally breaks free, dimples showing.

"West!" His friend calls out to him. Parker sits back in his seat, smiling to himself as the teacher begins to speak. His friends size me up, glaring. I just giggle as I look at the teacher.

Maybe Parker West isn't as cliché as people make him out to be.

"What are we doing in a plant shop?" I ask curiously.

"Number 20 on the list: Raised Anything Whatsoever. It doesn't matter, right? So we're going to raise a plant." He says.

"We're? Wow. Its always been my dream to be the baby mama of the Parker West's child." I say, faking a dreamy look and tone. He laughs and tugs me into isles. "I like that one."

I lie, pointing at some random plain green plant. He looks at me with a bored expression.

"We're getting you some flowers." He says. "Hmm. Flower. I like that nickname. It suits you. Come on, Flower." He says, testing it out. I shake my head as he pulls me into the flower section. Colors. A lot of them.

"Is this because my entire apartment is black and white?" I ask in monotone, not liking that he was mocking my bland style. He looks back, sending me a wicked smile that gave me all the information I needed. He picks up a red flower of some sort and tugs me by the wrist to the counter. The lady behind the counter looks down at it.

"Ahh, poppies are so pretty. Good choice." She murmurs.

"Yes, this adoption was very hard to think about. So many in so many different colors, shapes, sizes, beautiful all alike. We are honored to raise such a gorgeous child. Thank you so much, Ma'am." Parker says with a serious face and serious tone. She looks at him like he's insane, then glances at me.

"I'm sorry, Ma'am, he hasn't taken his meds today." I whisper loudly. He looks at me, slowly narrowing his eyes. Her eyes widen and she basically throws the now bagged plant at us. He catches it on instinct from being a basketball player. He grabs my wrist and drags me out.

"What the hell?!" He hisses at me. I shrug. "Your gonna pay for that later, but for now, we need to go shopping."

"What the hell?"

"Maybe they're expecting and they're practicing."

"Aww that's so cute!"

"I hate you. This is incredibly embarrassing." I mumble to him as he hums and pushes the stroller with our red poppies strapped inside, a pink blanket around the pot.

"Shh. Don't speak such crude words around Mila and Kila!" He hisses at me. I roll my eyes and shake my head.

"You... are a bit obnoxious, huh?" I state. He stops, so I do so too. He turns to me.

"Rude."

Then he continues pushing the carriage. I stand there, dumbfounded at his ability to not be offended by anything I insult him with, before he glances back at me with an impatient look. He motions for me to come over, but what he doesn't do is look at where he's going.

He trips on a ledge of a sidewalk thing, and goes flying to the ground, the stroller doing the same. Dirt flies all over him, and I burst out laughing. I even go as far as to slap my knee.

Knee-slapper indeed.

"O-oh my god!" I say between laughter's. People look at us as I slowly fall to the ground laughing, tears escaping my eyes. I hit the sidewalk with my fist, roaring with laughter.

"Shut up!" He hisses at me, scooping up dirt and putting it back in the pot.

"I-I HAH!" I let out, and fall into little giggles instead.

Slowly but surely, I get control again, and we start walking again as I wipe my tears.

Priceless. Gold. Vine-famous-worthy indeed. Funny funny funny.

I look at him, my lips pressed tightly to keep in laughter. Dirt remains on his shirt, his jeans now stained, some on his hair too. Finally, I laugh again, clutching onto his arm to keep from falling as I fall into a fit of laughter.

"Okay, Ally, we get it! Joke ended 5 minutes ago!" He shouts at me, causing me to laugh even harder. A smile tugs at his lips. "Really, you can stop laughing now." He says, and I start to gasp for air.

Finally, I get it out of my system.

"Wooh." I blow out an audible breath, then let one more laugh rise until it finally ends.

"Do you just like, love people getting hurt? Do you honestly take pleasure in that?" He asks. I grab onto the handles of the stroller.

I give him my best blank expression. "It turns me on." I tell him. His eyes widen. I start pushing the stroller.

"Are you serious?" He calls from behind me. I look back and smile.

I guess I shouldn't have done that.

Because next I know, the toe of my shoe gets caught on the sidewalk, and now I'm tripping. And now he's the one laughing. His laughter is so loud, that when I glance around, people are looking to him, then to me, and their eyes widen. People swarm around, helping me up ad glaring at him.

"What is wrong with you?! She could have gotten hurt!" Someone scolds him.

"Yeah she could have broken something!"

"You're so rude!"

"And you just stand by laughing? You're a sick human being!"

"How dare you!"

"Are you alright sweetheart?" someone asks. I place a hand to my elbow and hiss in pain when I touch some ripped skin that's bleeding, tears building up in my eyes.

"Aaawwww." A bunch of people coo at the same time.

"Baby. Its okay." And old lady says, pulling me in her arms. Parker looks confused as a crowd of fifteen verbally bash him for laughing at me tripping. She grabs band-aids from her purse and some cream and applies them. People pat my shoulders and give me their blessings before walking away with pitying looks and glares to Parker.

"Thank you." I tell the lady with a wobbly smile. She smiles back and pulls a lollipop out of her bag, giving it to me. I give her a hug in appreciation before she walks off. I glare at Parker while picking up the poor plant that bound to die all-too-quickly at this rate.

Finally my apartment building comes up as he walks silently behind me, muttering to himself about how double-standards are ridiculous and how women live life on easy mode. I roll my eyes and laugh, seeing as he's only jokingly upset.

When we get inside, I put the now disformed plant on the counter and water it, apologizing to them.

I open my lollipop and turn around, licking it as he glares at me, and he shakes his head twice.

"That's ridiculous. Where oh where is my crowd of beloved fans when I need them?" He ponders.

"I'm a nerdy looking girl with no taste in clothes. Your a guy that dresses like a total fuckboy and total overall douchebag." I state, motioning towards his khaki jeans and polo t-shirt, sported with a pair of black Jordan's. "Of course they're going to help me." I state, laughing a little.

He raises a finger, opening his mouth, but nothing comes out. He slowly lowers his hand, his mouth closing.

"Okay, I see your point. I'll get you for that too." He says. I snort. I turn around, shaking my head, repositioning the plant, and suddenly I'm picked up and thrown over his shoulders. He carries me into my room and throws me on my bed before walking to my closet. He opens it and pokes around. He tosses my brothers' old jersey before tossing me a pair of my cotton shorts and going to my shoe section. He lets out a whistle of appreciation upon sight of all of the basketball-made shoes.

"Damn," he says, "you should wear these more often." He says, picking up a pair of high tops and inspecting them. He picks up a pair of black and blue Adidas and tosses them to me, which I catch easily. "You like basketball?" He asks, still looking at the shoes.

I have a shoji binder in my room, so I tuck behind it so I can change without Parker seeing anything.

"Yeah." I answer, changing quickly.

"Best sport in my opinion." He says.

"Likewise." I say with a small smile before coming out. His eyes widen slightly and I grab a hair tie, slickly putting my dark hair into a high ponytail. Perks of having straight hair. So easy to work with.

"Jersey's suit you." He compliments as he grabs my wrist again and pulls me out. The second we reach the living room, the door of the apartment opens, and Laney and Sam enter. They both stop.

Silence.

"Uh." I say quietly.

A smile slowly grows over Laney's features.

"Don't even think about it." I tell her, knowing well about the Rylani fan page that happens to still be up and running. She pouts.

"Who's your friend?" She asks, holding out a hand to him. He shakes it quickly.

"Parker West. You know him." I say, waving a hand.

"..Parker... West.... Hmm... See, hold on, I don't pay much attention to other boys but Sam, so give me a second." She states. Sam gets a gleam in his eyes upon hearing that. She unknowingly probably just made his entire week with that sentence alone. "Oh! The basketball golden boy that everyone is obsessed with in my English class!" She states, seemingly recollecting her memory.

"That'd be the one." I say.

"Why are you here?" She asks in a serious tone, clearly confused. I let out a choking sound, a tragic laugh escaping my lips.

"Its a long story." I tell her. She smiles.

"Oh well. I don't care. Ally needs to get out more anyways. Have fun with your.. game I'm assuming because Ally goes to every single one." She says. "Psst, Parker," she says as we pass, "she has a sign with your name on it." She whispers.

"I do not!" I yell at her as he yanks me down the hallway. She peeks her head out, smiling wickedly, but I see Sam's arm wrap around her waist before he tugs her in forcefully.

Ew no thanks.

We talk about pretty much anything on the way to the field. Favorite colors: mine being blue, his being aqua green because he has an unhealthy obsession with Aquaman, favorite animals: mine being camel because I've always wanted to ride one, his being narwhal because of the song, favorite food: mine being chicken tenders because they're bomb, his being croissants because I guess he does a mean creepy French accent.

"Ready?" He asks.

Is he so oblivious to the crowd of guys watching us from the sidelines?

Is he really focusing on me that hard, or the game?

"I was born ready, West." I reply in a serious tone, taking a defensive stance, while still being casual about it, letting my shoulders back.

Do as your brother taught you, molded you to be.

Be the wiz at basketball you are.

Take out the college recruit.

He takes a rigid defensive form, one that's too rigid, way too rigid.

And the game begins.

Chapter 3

"I 'm going to destroy you." He states as he begins to dribble the ball. I smirk.

"Mm. That's where you're wrong." I state before surging forward, ducking under his arm and gaining control of the ball all in one swipe.

"OOH!" I hear his 'friends' yell out. He pays no mind.

"What the fuck...?" He murmurs as he turns to look at me. I giggle as I dribble the ball, moving backwards, using my tactic perfectly on him. "Short people, I tell you." He mutters.

"I am not short! Your the one that's 6'5" here, I'm 5'9" that's tall for a girl!" I hiss at him angrily. He shrugs.

"You do have a pretty nice pair of legs on you." He says, his gaze lowering.

"Step one in the game of ball: don't get distracted." I state as I toss the ball.

Soars over his head as he finally looks up with confusion, then, swoosh.

"You suck. You really do. That was... Stop." I say. I smirk in satisfaction at his dumbfounded expression.

"But I just.. I just looked for two seconds!" He hisses angrily.

"Two seconds is all it takes to lose, West!" I yell at him while running to the ball, bending down and grabbing it.

"Who is she?" I hear a voice bellow. I toss the ball to Parker while the metal gates open. The coach with a bunch of players come in.

"Oh, hey coach. This is my friend Ally. Ally, this is Coach Derek." He introduces.

"You dare insult one of my best players?" Coach asks. I shrug simply.

"One, your tactic on the game sucks, two, the way your coaching is just... Stop please, three, you're clearly not working hard enough because from what I've seen and what this season so far has seen alone.. Mm mmm mm." I say slowly, shaking my head. Some of the players try not to laugh.

"Oh and you think you could coach a bunch of college boys?" He challenges.

"Yes." I answer simply. His eyebrows raise.

"Alright, little Ally. Let's see what you've got. Boys, listen to her." He says.

A smile grows over my face.

When did my life get so interesting? Wasn't it just yesterday I was still sitting on my bed eating while binging Euphoria and secretly wishing I was Lexi?

"Alright, you four over there, you four over here." I say, making them separate. They go to either side. "Coach, why don't you take that team," I say, motioning to the left side, "and I'll take my side, and we train and by the end of the day we come back here and have a little match?" I offer. He purses his lips.

"Sure, sure." He says sarcastically. I look to the boys.

"Alright, come on. I have somewhere better to practice."

"What are you doing here, sis?" My brother asks as he leans against the doorway of his house - mansion - casually. He gives me a quick hug then I push him aside and lead the guys in.

"I have people to train. I have a match to do. Its a long story." I throw over his shoulder. "Hey Sally." I throw to his wife who smiles in return and follows him following the boys who follow me. They all look around.

I open the door to the private gym and let them in. They whistle in appreciation.

I lead them to the center of the gym.

"Now, first, I want you to stand in defense mode. Believe it or not, defense is one of the very most important things in the game of basketball, obviously." I say. I see Ty take a seat, Sally sitting on his lap. The guys - Danny, Parker, Leroy, and Jose - all take defensive forms. Me and Ty both put a hand over our faces. Sally giggles. I look up. "No, no, no." I mutter before walking over to the tool table. I grab the duck tape.

"What?" Parker asks.

"Shirts off." I command. They all smirk at the same time, doing the same slow motion ripping it off. I shake my head at their weak attempts to flash their muscles.

Though, Parker, when I see his muscles, this is what flashes in my mind: ok

I go behind them and begin putting waist trainers on them.

"What is this for?" Jose asks as I strap him up.

"This is to train your back." I answer, and go in front of them. I toss the tape aside onto a mat. "Now go back into your normal defense stances." I command. They all do so, and looks of discomfort begins to show instantly. "This is what I mean." I say. I go up to Parker and push on his shoulder to where it rolls back, and he's crouching more straight. I put my left hand to his waist and swallow as I move it forward slightly.

What can I say? I'm a sucker for a v-line on hips. Jeez. I step back. He looks a lot better.

"Still uncomfortable?" I ask. He shakes his head. The other guys' follow lead of the stance. My brother nods slowly from his seat. "Practice it, engrave this position into your soul." They start getting into the new and improved stance. My brother pulls me aside to his tool shelf and starts rummaging through.

"Leroy has an injury on his left knee, see it?" He asks. I look over and see it easily. Its painfully obvious. He looks as if he's putting all his weight into the right side of his body. "Tell him he needs to start going to physical therapy and to wear this during games." He says, handing me a knee brace. I nod and go to Leroy. He stops.

"Put this on your bad knee." I tell him. He nods and pulls it on. "You need to start going to physical therapy weekly, maybe twice a week, or you won't be able to play and you'll get permanent damage to your knee. Got me?" I ask. He nods quickly. "Keep going." I tell him. He smiles as he keeps doing it.

After a few minutes, I tell them to stop. I pull over the ball wrack. I toss them each a ball.

"Dribble." I command. They look at me weirdly. "Dr-i-bb-le." I say very slowly so they get it. They start.

"Really, I mean, dribbling is step one in basketball, Ally. How is this supposed to help?" Parker asks sarcastically.

"Its supposed to help because I want and need to go over every thing with you." I snap at him. He visibly cringes, looking as if regretting that question. "Leroy, don't put so much pressure on your lower back, straighten up." I tell him. He nods and does so.

"Yeah that feels a lot better on my knee." He comments. I smile.

"Jose, you on the other hand need to loosen up a bit. Along with you, Parker. Jose, put a slight bit of pressure on your lower back. Good. Okay, Parker, really. Just, loosen." I command. He does so. I walk forward and push his shoulders back to a normal and good place. I push his hips forward a tad bit and step back. I nod. "Just like that." I say with a smile.

"Danny, don't be so loose. Put a tad bit onto your lower back.. Yeah, now push your shoulders back a little. Yes, yes, yes. There we go, boys. Do this for ten minutes please." I state. I go over to the speakers and connect my phone. I turn on Spotify and turn on the 'Motivation' track list which starts with the song Purple Lamborghini.

I see the guys nod along to the song, getting more comfortable by the minute with how they're going.

Then, we're working on passes, then on shots, and finally jumps for finishing. When over, I give the guys drinks, and they all eagerly take them.

"Good job, sis." my brother says while passing with a light smile. Getting appraised by him sends pride bubbling through my chest. He's the only parent I ever knew, so it feels good.

He'd begun to raise me alone at 17. Our mother died giving birth to me, and our dad abandoned us because he blamed me for it. We'd started on the streets but soon Ty got a job and raised me. It'd been tough, but he went to college, and later became famous in modelling. Its weird seeing your brother half-naked on magazine covers, but that's how it is. I couldn't be more proud of him, though.

He'd always loved basketball passionately, and I personally believe he should be a coach - which he says he plans on being when modelling starts to fail - which drove him to build this gym in his mansion.

"You guys ready to kick some ass in an hour?" I hear Parker ask them. They all whoop.

"Hey, Ally, heads' up!" Parker yells. I turn at last second for the ball to hurtle into my stomach.

"OH FUCK!" I screech as I bend over in pain. It just slipped. I don't know how. I'd just completed a number on my list.

"WOOH NUMBER 24 COMPLETED BITCHES!" Parker yells out in glee. I glare at him.

"You better win this match you douche."

In the end, we did win. 1-9 because we were going 10 points in the game.

In the end, I was named Student Assistant Coach.

Chapter 4

"Come on, it'll be fun." Parker says, waggling his eyebrows.

"I'm tired." I whine. "How'd you even get in here?" I ask, already knowing the answer.

"I just told Laney I wanted you to be my companion to Coachella while it was still in town." He says with a cheeky smile. "I told her I thought you should get out. You've been working on the team for three days straight. As much as everyone appreciates it, you need a break." He says. He's right. I've been fixing the errors of their ways.

"Get ooooooouuuttt." I groan.

"Come on, I even got a makeup artist."

"Hey, I'm Connie." the woman pipes up finally.

One thing I notice.

She is defintely a he.

"Parkerrrrr." I whine as he pulls me out of bed. The Connie gives me a once-over before biting her fake nail.

"I'm thinking aqua to match her eyes." Connie says. Parker's eyes twinkle.

"Yes, yes, auqa is a good color."

"You just want aqua because of Aquaman." I glare at him. He shrugs.

"He's just so cool." He says. I laugh once. What a geek.

Connie and Parker lead me into the living room where two huge suitcases rest and a metal chair. Connie sits me in the chair before opening both of the suitcases. Laney sits on the couch on Sam's lap sipping wine as she giggles to herself.

It had to be Saturday.

As she begins to put some kind of 24-hour-only dye in my hair, I ask Parker a serious question.

"Why are you so obsessed with Aquaman?"

He looks at me as if I'm dumb. "Do you honestly see any other water or under the sea superheros that often? No. They're all from different planets or the Amazons or some shit." He informs me. "I like the uniqueness of him."

"What about Mermain Man and Barnacle Boy?" I ask, offended.

"Who the fuck?" He asks with a confused expression. My jaw falls slack.

"Only the best superheros to hit planet earth and T.V."

And that's how we wind up watching numerous episodes of Spongebob while I get my makeup done!

"Oh. My. God." I state while looking in the mirror. I mean, I hate overdone makeup, but damn do I like this Coachella makeup style.

I am feeling myself.

Parker comes in, and starts squealing like a maniac on meth. "Okay, I'm going to sound really gay right now, but bear with me. FUCKING SLAY. Girlboss." He says. I break into laughter.

"Oh my god that highlight is leaving me shook." He states in a try-hard girly and squeaky voice. I laugh again. "No but seriously, Aquaman would die for this. He'd smash." He says, nodding with a serious look on his face.

"Your so weird." I mumble.

"Come on, we got to get you dressed." He says, leading me to my own room. I shake my head as he starts opening drawers and my closet.

It isn't too long until he has an outfit. I have to admit, he pairs my own clothes better than I do.

I slip on some studded sandals and walk out. He nods as he gives me three once-overs before pulling me out. I grab my house keys. Laney raises her eyebrows.

"Looks amazing. Good luck in spotting LeLe Pons." She says, and I laugh.

"Like it'll be hard. She goes to every single festival."

"We got to stop at mine so I can get ready." he says, looking in the mirror. He too got a little bit of blue in his hair just for fun and so we'd match. Parker drags me out and we get in his car, a pretty black Nissan.

When we get to the apartment building, I look around. Its pretty. Really pretty. As we get in, I notice how it feels very warm and cozy, like people actually live there, unlike mine. Me and Laney keep it like no one's ever there.

I hear a child's squeal come from a different room.

"Sis?" He calls out.

I hear a woman's laugh. "I'm in here!" She squeals. He leads me to the room - the kitchen - where a woman that looks pretty similar to him - blonde hair and caramel eyes to die for- who I assume is his sister. A little boy who looks about a year old shoves cheerios in his mouth, then taking another one and throwing it at her. She giggles as she picks up the child's mess.

"What in gods name did you do to your hair, young man?" She asks in a stern voice. She doesn't look that much older than us, maybe 22, 23?

"Chiiiilill, it goes away in 24 hours." He says. She purses her lips.

"Better be because I am not walking around in public with Aquaman." She states. His eyes twinkle. Does she know she's creating fantasies in his head of being Aquaman? "Who's this?" She asks, her gaze turning to me. I fidget in my place nervously.

"This is my friend Ally who's borderline anti-social and doesn't go out much. I invited her to Coachella." He says freely, a joking smile on his face.

"I'm Milly, this idiot's older sister, and this cutie's mom. This is Jacob, my baby." She says, motioning towards the child. I shyly smile at them both.

"Nice to meet you." I say quietly. Something about her makes me want to make a good first impression.

"Come on, I gotta get ready. You're going to help me." He states, grabbing my wrist and tugging me.

"You're so pushy." I whine. I hear Milly laugh loudly from the kitchen at that statement. I look around his room as he closes the door. Band posters, a jacket draped over a chair to a computer set, two doors, one I'm assuming for a closet and one for a bathroom, dresser, bedside table, queen sized bed. I sit on his bed as he starts showing me clothes.

He wears mostly black. Black jean joggers, a back shirt that reads: Yeezus with a skeleton praying on it, a pair of black and aqua colored high tops, and to finish it, he puts an aqua colored bandana on.

"Perfect." He says in the mirror, running his hand through his hair before smiling in satisfaction. "Come on, if we want good spots, we gotta go." he says. I nod and we get to his car. "What is the song you've been humming while I got ready?" He asks. He plugs in his phone and hands it to me with YouTube open.

"You watch Shane Dawson?" I giggle out. He shrugs.

"I don't give a fuck that his fan base is 11 year old girls who are confused about their sexuality and constantly moody, that guy is funny." He states. I smile and nod before looking up Borderline.

We listen in silence, but his fingers tap on the steering wheel as we listen. A smile grows over my face as I look out the window, the beach passing by.

This is what excitement is.

No, this is what living is.

I'm sorry I took it for granted, Melinda.

What happens afterwards? When the list has been completed?

Dammit subconscious! Stop it!

Will you still talk? Will you still be friends?

Maybe, maybe not. Lets find out. I want to find out. Because I'm in for the long run.

"Oh my." I state as we step into the area. Its pretty filled, we struggle a bit to make our way to the front, but since we're incredibly early it isn't impossible. He puts up his chair while I put up mine. Just because we're going to be waiting for about four hours.

"Lets go ride a few rides. We can't ride too many because people will be coming in very soon." He says. I nod. "Hey, why don't we knock off number 28 off the list while we're at it." He offers. I feel myself pale. "It's fine. rollercoasters are perfectly safe. Plus, think about whatever reason you have for that list to be a thing." He says. I think about Melinda. I nod and he grabs my hand, leading me away. Melinda would want me to do this. She'd want me to live.

As we get closer to the machine, my nerves start to build up. At first, I'm about to flee, but then a sudden burst of determination courses through me. We get on, and my nerves build in my stomach as we strap in. I weave my fingers in with Parker's as it starts to move.

"You're perfectly safe." He reminds me.

It builds up, the rollercoaster, it builds with suspense. The kind of suspense in a book with a major plot twist that you never see coming.

Like when the author foreshadows it, and you see it coming, but its something insane that you never would have ever expected unless its a wicked cliché book.

Finally, we reach the top, and for a moment, time s t o p s.

I look around as it stops, the moment, I see everything in a new kind of light. We're so high up, I can see the Coachella stadium, I can see the rides, I can see Parker's widened eyes, sparkling with excitement, his smile brighter than the sun searing down on us right this moment.

Then its over and we're hurtling 83 feet to the ground, me screaming at the top of my lungs. Parker shouts in excitement. Another 30 people screaming and shouting.

Adrenaline courses through my veins, my bones, my heart.

My heart.

My heart has never beat faster than in this moment.

My head feels scattered as we're tilted upside down for a moment, even more adrenaline pumping.

A huge smile grows over my face. I love it. I love this.

For the first time in so long... I love life.

I feel it in my heart, my bones, my blood, my soul.

But all too soon, its over, and we're getting off, me with a giddy smile, high on life itself.

"Woah there." Parker says, catching me by the waist as I almost trip. A spark shoots through me. Must be the adrenaline. "You okay?" He asks.

"Yeah, yeah." I reply, looking up with a huge smile. A smile slowly grows over his face too. "Little lightheaded." I tell him. He leans down.

"Climb on my back." He tells me. I hop up and he carries me back to our seats. I laugh.

I secretly sniff his hair. Mmm. Vanilla.

"Did you just sniff me, Allison?" Parker deadpans.

"....Maybe."

He sets me down and we go.

We both get an aqua colored mini bear from some game and walk back to the concert we're attending. More people have showed up. We get to our seats, now with cokes in our hands and our bears, and sit. We talk, about nothing to everything. For hours, we enjoy each other's company.

This is what enjoying yourself feels like.

I smile.

Soon, we have to pick up our chairs and put them back in standing mode and putting them over the fence, because the show starts. It's exhilarating, this feeling of happiness, of excitement, adrenaline. It's almost drugging. At some point, Parker shouts over the insanely loud music and points behind us.

I look to see a blonde girl on a man's shoulders, and slowly I recognize her features.

LeLe Pons!

Chapter 5

"For the last time, Donte, square your shoulder more." I say, very tired. It has been a long week. Between having exams this week, basketball coaching, and sleeping, me and Parker haven't been able to do anything else yet. To be honest I was a little lonely this week with all the studying by myself. Parker had given me a taste of companionship and I didn't want the taste to end.

It was drugging.

He was drugging.

The bell rings. "Alright, boys, you know what that means, practice over, go home. Don't forget practice on Monday! We have our first game on Thursday!" Coach yells at them. He nods at me and I go to the changing rooms. I change back into normal clothes and sigh as I walk out.

"Boo!" Parker yells as I exit the locker rooms. I don't jump. I blankly stare at him.

"Not in the mood." I say emotionlessly and brush past him.

"It's like when I take a step with you, we take two steps back?" he says in a confused tone.

"No, no, I'm just tired. Studying, coaching, homework, an 1000 worded essay." I grumble.

"Thhhaaaaaattttt sucks, but guess what I got?" He asks, holding up a bottle with a wooden cork and a bunch of paper and a pen. "Come on." He says with a smile. I follow him to his car and sigh as my back hits the comfortable leather seat.

"Get it out." He says, plopping the stack of paper on my laps and handing me the pen.

Dear everybody and nobody,

Hey stranger. Wow, the term suddenly has a new meaning to me. I don't know who you are, but thanks for reading this little fun thing here. Trust me, it wont be fun, in fact this is going to be depressing, because I'm going to tell you the story of my life.

So let's take it all the way back to when I was a wee fetus. My mother died giving birth to me. My brother had been 17. My dad was so angry and blind with grief that he blamed it on me, so he left. I have yet to see him since, though he's tried contacting me.

So, my 17 year old brother grew up sooner than I wish he'd had to. He raised me, paid for my schooling, had about three steady jobs to pay for his own schooling along with paying apartment rent and food and bills. When his schooling was up, he got a call one day from a company named Rolex. He'd on a bet applied to be a model, and he didn't expect to get it because it was a joke, but he did. He is now known as the model Ty Smith. Pretty famous. He's happily married to his wife, Sally, who just got pregnant. He says when modelling starts to fail, he's going to become a basketball coach - what he'd studied for.

Have the camera shoot to me as an awkward teenager in high school that didn't quite suit her long legs yet and had a bad case of acne. (Luckily I filled in and my legs suit me, and my acne is cleared. It gets better, people... At least, that's what I thought...)

My only friends were an Asian girl named Sue and Melinda Compton. Melinda was very popular. She was perfection in its finest form, she was very kind, beautiful, got attention from men, with flowing blonde hair and sparkling blue eyes... You couldn't help but want to be her friend.

See, she'd done a lot with her life. I mean a lot. It included 50 things that she'd told me about that I'd written down as things I should find out what are like someday.

One week she was at a party. She found her best friend and her boyfriend hooking up. She'd been so in love with that boy, she told me it physically hurt. They called her names afterwards. She'd begun to have depression, which didn't suit her at all.

We'd begun talking a lot, and became very close friends. The day I was going to confront her about having painfully obvious depression was the day she committed suicide. I take the blame. I was too late. I should have helped sooner than I did.

Have the camera shoot to me for three years numbly walking the halls, depressed myself, contemplating suicide myself for something so terrible. When your best friend dies, you die. Understand that and pray it never happens.

I'd become even more anti-social.

Now have the camera shoot to about 2 weeks ago, when I'd decided to visit Starbucks. Where I dropped my list of things that she'd done that I never had. When the popular boy decided to help me succeed in completing the list.

For the first time in a long time I'm feeling what its like to live. Adrenaline is incredible, let me tell you. Try riding a roller coaster before going to a Coachella show. It's worth it.

That's it.

But I wonder what's to come when the list is complete.

Guess I'll find out.

Thanks for listening.

Bye.

"That's a long letter. What's it say?" He asks, trying to look. I fold it a few times.

"Nothing. Everything." I mumble before taking the bottle from his hands and putting it in there.

"A mystery. Come on, I wanna know." He says with a smile.

"I'll tell you another time." I mumble. His smile fades slowly and he takes the paper and the pen before writing himself. I look out the window, staring at the ducks as they swim by lazily. I see a seagull starts swooping to the ground to the direction of the baby ducks. Instantly I open my door and jump out as the seagull tries grabbing at one of the babies. I rip off my jacket and my shoes and jump in, swimming over to the duck that it bit. I pick it up, and the other ducks go away from me from fright.

"Poor baby. I'll help you." I whisper to the little yellow thing quietly upon seeing it have a little blood. Its also very dirty. I struggle swimming back and Parker helps me out of the water. The seagull is gone luckily. He grab my stuff, throwing them in the back of the car, and grabbing a blanket before wrapping it around my shoulders. I take my jacket and lightly place the baby duck inside to keep it warm. It stares up at me.

"Why'd you do that?" Parker asks as he closes the glass bottle and chucks it into the ocean.

"Because I didn't want it to die." I mumble as I sit in the seat. "Can you drive to a vet's office please?" I ask softly. He looks over and smiles.

"Of course.. You know, you sell yourself short, I think. You're an amazing person." He states. A bubbling feel erupts in my stomach and I smile down at the baby duck.

"Maybe I can keep you, like they did in Friends." I suggest. It opens its mouth and a little sound comes out. "Awww oh my god you're so cute." I coo, petting its little head with one finger.

"You should name it." Parker suggests.

"If your a boy, Jordan, if your a girl, Addy." I murmur.

"Really? Jordan and Adidas?" Parker asks, laughing. I nod.

"Best shoes ever."

We pull into a little vets place and I walk in awkwardly. People's eyes widen upon a drenched girl coming in with a baby duck in her hands who's little baby neck is bleeding. "Hi, I just saved this little duck from a seagull that was attacking it, and it's neck is bleeding." I tell her. The woman nods and writes something down.

"Take a seat and we'll be with you soon." She says with a smile. I hand the jacket with the baby duck, and he smiles down at it. What a sight.

"I have a set of your clothes on my backseat." Parker tells me. My eyes widen, and I step back once. "Chill! I was going to push you in the lake as a prank.. Didn't work."He mutters. I laugh and make my way outside. I get in his backseat and change in there. The dude had the nerve to touch my under-garments.. ooh he's dead.

Worst thing is, he grabbed a pair of black, lacy satin under-wear and its matching bra. He couldn't grab a normal cotton set? He had to go for the lingerie? The nerve of men these days, I swear.

I pull on the black leggings, gray t-shirt and olive green bomber jacket he had put back here and I laugh once as I pull on my shoes.

He's dead.

I step out, feeling a lot better. I make my way in to see a man carefully taking the duck, and a little girl 'aww'ing. We follow the man in because they said we could.

They wind up shaving a little part of his cute little yellow fur so they can see. Not bad, just needs a little patch. They give him a dawn bath and put the little patch on him. I pay for the expenses and take the little thing back.

"Hey, by any chance is it a he or a she?" I ask. The doctor smiles at me.

"He."

"Thank you." I say before walking towards the door. Someone stops me. I look over to see an old woman holding an old cat.

"Bless you for saving the little one's life." She says. I smile and nod, thanking her before walking out. Parker has a smile on his face.

"Always an interesting day where you're concerned." He says. I laugh.

"Up for more shopping?"

"Mm. I don't know. I think sea foam is just a little too... eh.. The aqua one is better anyways." He says as we look at fabric. I know how to sew, so I'm going to make little sweaters.

"We need other colors than just aqua, Parker. Jordan doesn't need to be ridiculed for wearing the same thing every day. Plus, red looks good too." I say while I put some red and aqua fabric in the cart on his arm. Jordan squawks in my arms. "Ooh little beige sweaters." I coo as I grab some beige fabric.

"Ooh black." Parker says, grabbing some. I nod. "Maybe some navy blue too?" He offers, holding it up. I nod.

Luckily, I already have a sewing machine at the apartment.

"I think we're good." I say, grabbing double of each color we'd picked out for when he starts to grow. We check out and chat as we get back to the car. Soon enough, we're at Walmart looking at baby things.

"I think we should go with the aqua colored crib."

"Goddammit, Parker, not everything has to be aqua!" I exclaim. I see a family eyeing us, stopping just to watch. Jordan quacks in my arms. I hold him up. "Oh I'm sorry baby.

Me and daddy are just fighting on which crib to buy you. Your gonna be a spoiled little baby, yeah." I say softly, nuzzling my nose into his neck. He's so soft.

"Think about it, aqua is the color of the sea and the sea is where he comes from so he'll be more comfortable." He says. I sigh.

"Fine." I let up. He smiles and grabs two of the cribs. We're splitting expenses here because we're both buying two of everything. I grab a stray bib that has a duck on it. I toss it in. Jordan rests in my left hand. "We need sturdy strollers, not plastic toy ones." I tell him. He nods and we go down the isle. I get a black stroller and he of course gets the color closest to aqua. We both buy a kitty pool each.

"Awe, honey, look." I hear a woman whisper. I turn slightly and see an old woman pointing at us. "They're having a family and preparing." She gushes. I smile at her, and hold up Jordan, who quacks at them. The old man bursts into laughter as his wife jumps in shock.

"We already are a family." I tell her with a smile. "Adopted." I state. Technically we did. We went to the ASPCA and got forms and everything. Luckily, our apartment building lets animals allowed. We continue.

His car is basically filled, and he calls up a few of his friends to help unload seeing as I'm not just going to set Jordan down on the street while we unpack.

We get my half of the stuff out and they bring it inside. Parker shuts the car trunk and follows in.

When we all come in, Laney looks shocked as hell.

"What..?" She trails off. I walk up to her.

"This is Jordan, mine and Parker's baby duck whom I saved from a malicious seagull. I have custody on weekdays, he gets him Fridays through to Monday morning." I inform her. She looks at me like I'm insane before reaching out and petting him. She smiles and shakes her head.

"You... I'm not even going to comment anymore." She says before going to her room. I have the guys take the stuff into my room.

Like said, apartment is big, so we have no trouble adjusting furniture to where my bed is in one corner, the crib is in the other, the kitty pool is leaning against the wall beside the crib, and the stroller is propped up against the wall. I set Jordan in the little bed and he quacks before laying down.

"Thanks guys." I say to the boys and grabbing my bags of material. I go to the little table with the sewing kit and get to work as Parker and the guys' talk. Parker takes a picture of Jordan, saying this is going to get - and I quote - a bunch of chicks.

"We are not using my child as a babe magnet." I pipe as I finish the first mini sweater to fit the ducks' body. Leg holes, wing holes check, backside missing any fabric because I'd rather not have little duck feces stains on the sweater, and I pick up Jordan. Parker helps me put it on him, and I smile as I put him back in. He takes another picture.

I continue to make duck sweaters and slowly, one by one, Parker's friends leave. Parker lays on my bed with a smile on his face as he stares at the ceiling.

"Life has been more amusing since we met." He states. I look over at him.

"Likewise." I reply, accidentally nicking my finger. I hiss in pain for a second, sucking the blood before going back to the sweater before I mess it up.

After I'm done with that one, I shut the machine down. 11 little sweaters. I give him 6 of them, making sure to give him mixed colors. He smiles.

He stands, saying he needs to sleep before the game tomorrow, and I lead him out.

I lean against the door, watching him walk away.

"Hey, Ally?" He asks, turning around for a second. "Thanks." He says.

"For what?" I ask, slightly confused.

"For making it less lonely for me."

Chapter 6

"Come on... Come on..." I say over and over as Parker goes forward with the ball. Everyone on the team has improved very nicely. It's the final score of the game. In the last few seconds, Parker jumps and dunks it. I spring up, screeching at the top of my lungs along with about 200 other people, though I'm sitting like V.I.P. next to the coach.

I even got a jacket and everything.

It's announced we won, and Parker runs to me and engulfs me in a sweaty hug. I laugh and hug him back. "That was amazing!" I squeal in his ear. His arms tighten, my heartbeat picking up at the proximity.

"It's all because of you, Flower." He says, and I smile into his neck. Why does he still smell like vanilla when he's covered in sweat? How? Why? How come I can't do that?

"I have a surprise for you," I inform him. He leans back.

"YEAH WEST, GET IT!" His friend shouts, slapping his back. I feel my cheeks heat up.

"Not that kind of surprise!" I hiss at Leroy. He laughs freely and walks away.

"Alright. Let me shower and change quickly." He says before running to the locker room with a smile, and a boyish gleam in his eyes. After about twenty minutes, he comes out smelling even more vanilla than before! What does he use?!

I grab his wrist and tug him out back, where the hot air balloon sets in the huge field. His jaw drops before it turns into a huge smile.

"Oh my god!" He basically screeches out. There's a person to handle it waiting inside, reading. She looks up and drops the book. I lead Parker in and the lady starts telling us to hold on. Parker is wicked excited.

I grab Parker's hand as we start to go up, scared.

"It's okay, Ally." He comforts. He draws me to his side as we go higher and higher. Higher than a Ferris wheel.

The adrenaline, the rush coursing through my veins.

"YEEAAAAH BITCHEEEES!" I scream at the top of my lungs. I look down and try not to have a heart attack and see people looking up at us.

Suddenly, arms wrap around my waist and lift me in the air. I scream as Parker puts me slightly over the edge. He booms with laughter as he puts me back down.

"YOU'RE FUCKING DEAD, PARKER!"

As we land safely on the ground, a few of the basketball guys - aka Parker's friends watch us, I start slapping Parker repeatedly.

"YOU-" slap, "COULD-" slap, "HAVE-" slap, "KILLED-" slap, "KILLED-" slap, "ME YOU NEANDERTHAL!" I scream at the top of my lungs. "You don't pick a girl up and put her over the edge of A HOT AIR BALLOON!" I scream even louder.

"Daaaaamn. Hitting you with her sexy little nerd words, Parker. She mad." Leroy says.

"Oh fuck off, Leroy. Do you want to be off the team, and kicked off your scholarship?" I ask, glaring at him.

"It's like ever since you got her to say 'fuck' she can't stop saying it," Ty says, shaking his head. I narrow my eyes at him next. "Sorry, Ma'am." he squeaks instantly. I open the door thing and step out.

"Useless... Fucking... Hormonal, perverted.. little.. boys.. can't.. do. anything right? And we're the ones.. who don't deserve constitutional rights... What kind of bullshit is this? Men do everything.. wrong.." I mutter angrily while Parker follows me silently, walking strangely, almost like a duck, waddling. "Even.. getting walking wrong." I spit angrily to myself, and Parker stops and walks normally.

"I thought it was funny." He says in a sheepish tone.

"What, your walk, or holding me 100 feet to my death?" I ask, glaring at him, my head turned to look.

Aaaand I probably should stop paying so much attention to him, because the next thing I know, I'm tripping. Again.

And he laughs again. So, I grab his ankle as he moves to walk away, and tug, him tripping in resulting right on that sexy little face of his.

"You're.. a real bitch.. you know." Parker heaves as he lifts himself by his elbows. I spring up and kick him in the leg, and he falls again. "OW! WHAT WAS THAT FOR?!" He shouts.

"For being an asshole!" I yell at him. To the side, two young girls are stopped mid-step, Starbucks both about to be taken a sip of. "Need something?" I ask kindly, and they both start giggling.

"Couple. Goals." They both say at the same time. Their phones are in their hands, pointed at us. Great, recording.

"Just be sure to blur my face!" Parker yells.

"We're not a c-"

Parker grabs my ankle and pulls me, me ending up falling on him as result. "HA! I had a pillow, you dimwit!" I yell in glee. He just looks at me with widened eyes. His eyes scan my face. "Uh-"

"WOAH! What did we walk in on, boys?!" I hear the voice of Braden, the douchiest of all of them. Braden was notorious for being an asshole, aggressive, picking fights, etc. He was known for harming women as well. Myself included.

I get off of Parker instantly.

"I, I think Parker boy was about to get some with the nerd!" Braden says, and the other douchebags around him start laughing as Braden smirks. I tuck hair behind my ear and look at the ground, my face heated up. Parker looks at me as if confused. "She good in bed, P?"

Parker continues to stare at me with his eyebrows scrunched together.

"I'm gonna go.." I whisper und wave my hand awkwardly in front of me before pointing behind me with my thumb. I turn on my heel and start speed-walking away.

"Shut up, Braden. Stop being a douche." I hear Parker snap at him before footsteps start to be sounded behind me. I walk faster so he can't catch up. Damn jocks. Always gotta ruin everything for everyone, right?

His footsteps speed as well before we're both walking into the school, out of sight from Braden and the rest. Hands clamp down on my shoulders and turn me to him.

"Hey, hey, what's wrong? What was that? Why didn't you stand up for yourself? You never.." He trails off, shaking his head.

"I can't... I... I just want to go home." I whisper. His eyes scan my face again.

"Did he do something to you?" He asks. I glance around.

"Parker... I just... You bring out a side of me only a few see." I lie straight to his face, and I have to admit, it was the hardest thing I have ever done in my life; lie to Parker. Why? Why is that so hard?

"I don't believe you, or that... But.. I'll let it go. For now." He says softly. I nod and look down as a tear falls. He wipes it away and pulls me in for a hug. I wrap my arms around him and breathe in his vanilla scent, calming down instantly. "Come on, let's go watch a movie with Jordan."

"For real? After torturing me with all High School Musicals, both Mean Girl movies, and that trash movie Be Someone, do you want to watch yet another? Safe Haven? What even ...?"

"Shut up! Safe Haven is amazing. I promise it's better than all of the movies we just watched - other than High School Musical, because, I mean, what beats that? Also, ew your jacket is so out."

"You're acting like Regina and I don't like it!" Parker shouts at me. Our neighbors must be very confused.

"Okay, it's not my fault I was raised to be a savage. God. Get it right." I snap at him. "And FYI, the color aqua died in the summer of 2014, leave it there, please."

"Oh, you did not just offend aqua."

"Oh yes, I did."

"You are not going there." He says, shaking his head.

"Oh yes, I am." I snap my fingers.

"Would you both shut the fuck up?" A new voice joins in. An unfamiliar one. I turn around to see Laney, Sam, a black-haired guy I've seen in pictures, and that blonde chick I see in pictures often wearing crop tops and ripped jeans. "I'm sorry, but I had to." The blonde says.

"Uh... So, Kehlani, Ryder, this is my roommate and her... Friend? I don't know... Basketball golden boy thing named Parker who's very annoying. They are raising a plant and a baby duck together and pretending to be parents with them. Ally, this is Kehlani and Ryder, the ones we told you about." Laney lets out a breath when she's done.

"Nice to meet you," Kehlani says with a warm smile. She holds out a hand to each of us, and we shake it. "Usually I'm not so crude anymore but loud noises set me off, and well, you guys were screaming at the top of your lungs." She says, laughing a bell-like laugh at the end.

I don't know why, but she seems like the type people would mesmerize over, maybe even worship.

"Pleasure to meet you." The black-haired guy - Ryder- says, smiling just as warmly. What the hell is it with attractive people always dating attractive people?! At this rate, I'll never get a boyfriend! Ryder takes Kehlani's hand and she - from what I can tell - subconsciously leans to his body. Almost like magnets. Weird.

"Did you just see that?" Parker asks me, narrowing his eyes at Kehlani. She gets a confused look. I look at him.

"What?" I whisper.

"Her body. It just.. Moved towards him." He says.

"Yeah, I saw that too!" I whisper back. "It's like.."

"Magnets." He finishes the sentence for me. We look each other in the eyes and start nodding slowly. Suddenly, a squawking noise raises in the air, followed by three more. Me and Parker sigh and get up, heading to my room. We get Jordan dressed in a little red outfit and walk out. I hold Jordan in my arms as Parker coos, petting his head.

"You weren't lying," Kehlani says as we walk out. We both look up with a smile.

"We're like a divorced family, only we were never together, to begin with," Parker says. I laugh once.

"Why do you both have bruises on your faces?" Laney asks curiously. We all move to the kitchen. Parker gets Jordan his little meals of sardines in a can and seeds and puts him on the counter. He cuts the sardines in half so it's easier, and Jordan starts eating while everyone looks in disgust. I smile at Jordan as he mutilates the fish, along with Parker.

"So cute." Parker and I together, and smile at each other before looking back at our baby.

"We have bruises because we both often fall and trip each other on cement," I answer the previous question.

Parker's eyes suddenly light up. Uh oh.

"I HAVE AN IDEA!" He yells at the top of his lungs, causing everyone but me to jump in shock.

"What?" I ask.

"Let's throw a party on the roof! We can knock two off your list! Number 2 and number 16!" he says gleefully. "Wait, but I suck at throwing parties. And you wouldn't be good either." He tells me, offending me, but I get it.

Everyone looks at Laney, who looks at Kehlani, who has a creepy, dark, smile slowly creeping over her face.

"I'm in." That is all she says.

May I repeat?

Uh oh.

Chapter 7

"Alright, I'm done," Kehlani says. I gape at the cart filled with Chinese lights, some of the Chinese lamps that fly away too, snacks, dips of all sorts, plastic silverware, paper plate stacks, and much more. I look up at her. "Ready?" She asks. Ryder comes up behind her and wraps his arms around her waist, putting his head in the crook of her neck.

Oh my god. They are so cute. I can't even.

"I don't like you throwing parties." Ryder sighs into her neck. Her face softens. I look away awkwardly, sensing the story behind this.

She smiles at him and pushes the cart into the check-out lane. "Not like Andrew's around to bother me anymore." She says, smiling at him widely as his eyes storm over. She grabs his hand, and his anger diminishes instantly. We all help put the stuff up.

"What are you kids doing?" The lady at the desk asks.

"I'm throwing my first party with the help of my new acquaintances," I tell her.

"HEY LOOK THE NERD!"

"THAT'S IT! YOU WANT TO LOSE YOUR SCHOLARSHIP TOO, TY?!" I screech back at him. The lady looks shocked. "Sorry, I have no clue why he's here. It seems basketball players take the joy out of following me around." I tell her. Her face shows concern.

"Are they stalking you? I could call security." She says. I laugh.

"No, no. It's fine." I say with a smile. Ty and Leroy finally turn up.

"Oh, who's the babe?" Ty asks, looking over at Kehlani. Ryder pulls her to him possessively. "Ha, dude, I'm messing with you. Pullin your leg. Saw ya looking at her. I'd know that gaze anywhere. It's the same little gaze our friend gives his little crush." Ty says, punching my arm lightly. I narrow my eyes.

"I'm considering kicking you off of my team," I growl out.

"You're not the coach." He says with a cocky smirk.

I step up and look him in the eyes.

"I'm an assistant coach with a famous brother who can make quite the convincing case when I think something doesn't belong. Try me, Tyler, try me." I say in my lowest voice possible. He steps back, his hands up. I drop the act and smile. "Also, party at my place, on the roof, at 8 o'clock. Be there or be a loser!" I say brightly, then swipe my card through the scanner to pay for all of the things before Kehlani does. She blinks, and then slowly puts her card away.

"I'll be there. Bring a few of the boys, too?" He asks.

"Everyone but Braden and his posse," I told him darkly. He blinks, looking confused.

"Why? They're awesome at a party-"

"Braden Lilick better not even step foot on my apartment's complex. He shouldn't even know. Don't fucking tell him. I don't want to deal with that douchebag." I snap at him. He raises his hands.

"Fine, fine, just a couple of close friends then." He says. I nod. "Alright, alright, I got you. See you later then." He says, and they walk off.

"Speaking of Braden, ready to tell me?" Parker asks. I shake my head and he nods. I wave to the cashier before Parker pushes the cart. I run ahead of the cart suddenly and step onto the little thing on the bottom so I can ride it while he pushes. "Daaaamn. How much do you weigh?!" He asks.

"Shut up. I'm legit 110 pounds."

He stops the cart.

"Your underweight. Are you okay? Are you eating enough? Do you have an eating disorder? Have you ever had an eating disorder? Are you okay? Don't say you're fine, because I read online that when girls say they're fine, it means the opposite."

"Damn you really are annoying," Kehlani says before walking ahead of us, arm linked with Ryder who seems to follow her like a puppy. Again. Cute.

"Parker, I'm f-"

"Don't say fine."

"Fine. I never really had a large appetite and have always been a bit skinny. Not to where my ribs show or anything, but yeah. Yeah, you get it." I mutter the last part.

"You better not be lying," he says, his eyes starting to narrow. I shake my head with a smile. I turn to see Kehlani forcefully push Ryder on the hood of her awesome sports car and hold his arms down while she kisses him.

Oh my. Is she a dominatrix?

"STOP!" Sam yells at them. She pulls back and sends a smirk in our direction. Ryder looks dazed. We all make our way to our respectable cars, and get in. On the way back, Parker sings Closer at the top of his lungs, then the song I'm Poppy, which... I don't even...

When we get back, we all grab bags and head up to the roof.

After about two hours of crying on my behalf of how many times I trip over cords from the lanterns and Parker dancing like people out of Charlie Brown's Christmas, we're finally done.

"Turn the lights down now, now I'll take you by the hand. Hand you another drink, drink it if you can. Can you spend a little time? Time is slipping away. Stay with me I can make-make you glad you came." Kehlani sings along in a perfectly, angel-like voice, slightly moving as if she wants to grind on someone. I see Ryder eyeing her. I push him towards her, and they sing along together, swaying against each other's bodies. Sam looks disgusted and goes back to stapling the last light properly.

"The sun goes down, the stars come out. And all that counts is here and now. My universe will never be the same."

I walk to the edge of the roof's glass barrier to keep people from falling which is around the entire thing on stone and look at the city around us. Parker stands next to me with a smile. "I'm glad you came. I'm glad you came."

I'm glad, very glad, that Parker came into my life.

"Thank you, Parker." I whisper after the song had just ended.

"My heart's a stereo, it beats for you so listen close. Hear my thoughts in every note." the new song starts up.

"For what?" He asks with a smile.

"Getting me out more. Doing what you're doing for me. I mean, you're taking most of the time out of your days with me now." I say shyly. "Thanks."

He nudges me with his elbow. "No problem, Flower. Plus, you're more fun than Braden Lilick." He says jokingly. People now have shown up as I glance behind us. About twenty people are in, and more are coming through. I grab his wrist and pull him out, ignoring Laney's whoop about getting 'dicked down'.

"Where are we going?" he asks. I pull him into the apartment and sit him on the couch and sit across from him.

"I... I might as well just tell you my issue with Braden." I tell him. He rests a hand on my knee, giving a sign of comfort if needed.

"You can tell me." He whispers.

"It was about a year ago. I was walking in the hallway after school, I stayed after late in the library. It was around nine." I tell him. I glance up to see his face look like it break.

God. He's jumping to conclusions higher than a kangaroo.

"He came up out of nowhere and shoved me to the wall.. Uh.. His hands kind of.. Wandered. I kept telling him to stop, and he'd just keep complimenting me over random things. I tried pushing him off. He grabbed my... Well... Uh... Chest? I kicked him in the balls and ran away. I got away safely. And uh- I'm fine. I just.." I shake my head.

He pulls me into his arms. "I'm going to fucking kill him." He says in a dark voice, sounding angry, which is something I thought I'd only hear if I offended the color aqua again.

"I-its fine, Parker, really. I'm over it. I just hate him ever since... He kind of scares me." I admit.

"Don't be scared anymore. I'm here now."

But for how long, Parker? How long?

The drama started about an hour into the party, because it wound being that Braden Lilick decided to show up. I stopped Parker instantly, and we were talking when Braden came up out of nowhere and slung his arm around Parker's shoulder.

"Sooo, Parker," he says. His voice is not slurred. "How did you manage to score the nerdy babe, and I couldn't get anything?" He ponders. Parker's jaw locks.

"Maybe because I wasn't a fucking douchebag!" Parker growls, pushing Braden off of him. Braden takes a step back with his eyes widened, shock on his face.

"Woah, woah, buddy. What's wrong?" Braden asks innocently. Next thing I know, Parker is tackling Braden to the ground, people jumping back in shock.

"YOU-" punch, "FUCKING-" punch, "LAY-" punch, "ANOTHER-" punch, "HAND-" punch, "ON-" punch, "MY-" punch, "GIRL-" punch, "I'LL FUCKING KILL YOU!"

I am now crying.

I'm scared. Braden is out cold, blood trickling from his forehead and his now split lip.

Parker gets pulled off of him, faces me, and instantly pulls me into his arms. He picks me up bridal style and carries me out quickly. We get in my apartment, and he puts me on my bed. He sits next to me.

"I'm so sorry... I just couldn't..."

"Its okay, Parker." I whisper. He looks up. "Go get a bottle of whiskey from the cupboard." I demand. He raises his eyebrows but goes and comes back with two glasses and a half-filled bottle. He pouts two glasses and tries to hand one to me. I grab the bottle and start chugging it. When I finally stop chugging it, it burns my throat, and I start coughing, laughing at myself. He chuckles beside me.

"Be glad its only Friday." He says. I raise the bottle before tipping it back again.

That's two more.

I hope.. I hope he'll stay longer than the list.

Chapter 8

PARKER's POV

I woke beside her, this morning.

Why did it jolt my heart in a good way to see her there beside me?

I slowly get out and smile at the sleeping duck in his crib. Like a little family.

I smile to myself and walk out. On the couch is Kehlani passed out, Ryder slowly putting a blanket over her while setting a bucket next to the couch. He grabs the damp cloth off of his lap and lightly washes over her face.

"You really love her, don't you?" I ask quietly, not to scare him. He looks over with a smile.

"First time I laid eyes on her. My baby's been put through a lot, been broken, but I make sure she knows I'll always be there to pick up the broken pieces." He says and looks back down at her. He takes her hand in his and runs his hand over the ring on her ring finger - on an engagement ring. I smile.

"How'd you guys meet?" I ask, taking a seat on the chair.

"Seventh grade, I walked into the cafeteria with her twin brother - my best friend - and he pointed at her and told me who she was. I remember her look... I instantly just.. Knew. My heart just.. Stopped... When she caught our looks directed at her, she raised a perfect eyebrow, looked me up and down with a very calculating gaze, as if trying to figure out the type of person I was just by appearance, and then she smiled. I was gone just like that." He says, laughing once at the end quietly, holding her hand up and kissing it. He looks at me, and I see Kehlani smile before she masks it.

Ahh, she wanted to hear that.

Why does he remind me of myself?

Well, then again, Ally brings out a side of me I'd buried when I was twelve..

"You like Ally, right?" Ryder asks. My eyes widen.

"N-no!" I sputter out instantly. I just met her a few weeks ago! You can't just catch feelings for someone that quickly!

Can you?

He smiles.

"Deniaaaaal," Kehlani says from her sleeping spot in a sing-song voice. "Trust me, been there, done that, now I plan on marrying and creating a life with that." She says in a chirpy tone.

"I-uh-"

"Give it a rest, Kehls," Sam says from the side.

"I didn't tell you to listen about my love life with my fiancé." She says with a cocky smirk. She's a girl with a bad look, you can tell in her eyes she's seen some shit, been through stuff, and dealt with it the hard way.

Sam shakes his head.

"I hate this. I really do. Its... it's so wrong. Bro-codes broke n... Sibling-code broken... I. I just.." Sam trails off, and Laney comes up behind him, wrapping her arms around his torso and putting her chin on his shoulder.

"Need I remind you that you're doing the same thing, Sam?" Kehlani asks.

Ooooh. Sibling drama. These is straight goals. Best-friend-sibling-relationship things. Cute, cute.

"Uuuuum. Excuse me. She was my crush before she was your best friend thank you very much." Sam states, then his eyes flash and he blushes. Blushes. I start laughing at his expression, and others join. Laney leans up and kisses his cheek.

"Aww, baby, I'll be sure to buy you the pretty flowers that you want later." She says in a mocking tone, pinching his cheeks. He swats her hands away, and she takes it upon herself to spank him as she passes by. He yelps.

Suddenly, a screech comes from Ally's bedroom. I instantly run over, to see one baby duck named Jordan on her chest, snuggling into... Well.. The center gap. I laugh loudly.

Someone learned how to fly.

ALLY's POV

"This is insane. You're insane. Really? I don't think I'm ready for this, not this."

"It's okay, I'll make sure it doesn't hurt you too badly." He tells me with a reassuring smile.

"But.. I don't want to be sore tomorrow. We have plans.." I trail off.

"You guys realize that this sounds wrong, right?" Kehlani asks with a smirk. I go back over the last few words, and gag.

"What does sleeping with me sound that bad?" Parker asks, looking genuinely hurt. Fear that he's going to leave or walk away builds in my chest.

"U-uh no no! I-I didn't mean it like t-"

"Calm down, Al. I'm messing with you. So you'd smash, right?" Parker asks the façade dropping, his ears perking back as his killer dimples make their appearance. My cheeks start to creep with heat.

I tackle it down, my slight anger and new-found confidence getting rid of the heat. I smirk at him.

I step forward, placing a hand on his chest. "Uh... Ally.." He trails off. "What are you-"

"Yeah," I whisper, "I'd smash," I say, tapping my fingers on his hard chest. He swallows, looking... Nervous? I start laughing as I step back, laughing hysterically. "Oh my god, Parker. I'm messing with you!" I giggle. This time, heat creeps up his cheeks. He pushes into the tattoo parlor, and we all follow. I'm the last one in.

I notice a group of girls staring at us, crouched down as if to hide. The lead one sports an American flag bomber jacket. What in the world..?

"Ally, come on!" Parker calls in an aggravated voice. I laugh and ignore the people, going in.

See, it isn't a normal tattoo parlor. It isn't even a store. It's Parker's friend's house which tattoos people for fun. It doesn't even have a sign. You just gotta know him.

"So how many people want tats?" The guy that looks like someone out of a music video for Bad and Bougie asks.

"I do," Kehlani says, attracting the gazes of Sam and Ryder both. Laney doesn't look shocked.

"Me too," Laney says. Sam's gaze whips over to her.

"But your perfect skin! You must not taint it!" Sam says. Laney glares at him.

"I do too," I state. The guy looks over every one of us.

"Three hot chicks at once. Lucky day." The guy says with a smile before showing us some of the designs. Kehlani decides to get her current tattoo removed, and have it replaced with Ryder's name along with whatever scar is on her back. His eyes light up. Laney decides to get a shoulder tattoo, a large flower with roots twisting out, and I simply decide on a duck as a tramp stamp.

That's right.

A duck tramp stamp. Well, a duckling.

He decides to do mine first since it's the smallest. I lift my shirt a little and brace for the pain, but it doesn't come because the door is burst open, followed by a pride-full "AHHHA!"

"What the hell?" The bad-and-bougie guy who goes by the name of Bobby queries.

"Oh.." The girl standing there with a leather jacket says with a disappointed expression. She turns to the girls behind them. "Sadly they aren't having group sex."

"Liv?" Kehlani asks, her eyebrows raised. The girl, Liv, turns around slowly, with a pained expression. "Giana? Even you,

Laila? Really? Did you guys for real follow me?" She asks, giggling. Liv takes in the scene and amount of people.

"Weeeeelll." The girl with the prettiest deep red hair I've ever seen says. "Liv made us." She says, pointing at flag-girl.

"Are you... You're cheating on us?" Liv asks with a horrified expression. "Y-your hanging out with other people. You're cheating on us!" Her voice raises. Suddenly, a sharp pain hits my lower back, and I yell in pain.

"A LITTLE WARNING WOULD HAVE BEEN NICE!" I screech at the guy.

"Sorry." He mutters, continuing. I try my hardest to focus on the people, and not the excruciating pain.

"This is my brother and his girlfriend, Liv. I just met these two yesterday. I'm not cheating on you." Kehlani says with a confused expression.

"Did you just introduce me as your brother's girlfriend?" Laney asks, a hurt look on her face.

"S-sorry. I mean my best friend who happens to be my brother's girlfriend." She fixes herself.

"So you are cheating on us."

"NO! God, you're all my side-hoes, okay?! Ryder is my main bitch, and the rest of you are side-hoes." She yells out, clearly aggravated. Ryder looks at her.

"I'm hoping my competition isn't Liv. Wait. She has a boyfriend. So what, we're all side-hoes to each other?" Ryder asks, looking at the group, who all shrug.

"This is what we signed up for when I said squad goals, idiots. God. Whatever. Now that I know that you are and aren't cheating on us at the same time, is there any place close by I can start a riot at?" The strange flag girl says. Parker smiles.

"You're cool," he says. "I like the flag stuff, but instead of the dark blue, you should get it in aqua blue." He says. She looks down at her jacket before back up to him. Her eyebrows raise and she gets a thinking gaze as she nods slowly.

"You're right." She says.

"Always am."

"Same."

"Twins."

"Same."

"We must be long-lost twins. We should get a DNA test. But wait, I already have a twin brother..."

"TRIPLETS!" They both yell out. Bobby slightly jumps, and I yelp in pain, and he apologizes instantly.

"Parker... I'm... Going.. to... K-kill you!" I hiss slowly through gritted teach.

"We even both have brown hair. Wait but your eye color is brown. Mine's blue." She says. "But my mom's eyes are blue!" She says. He nods. "She'd be willing to accept you into the family." She says. His eyes light up.

"I've always wondered what having a mom would be like." He says wistfully, clasping his hands together. He never had a mom too?

Does everybody not notice Kehlani slowly leading Ryder to the bathroom?

Ew. Not the tattoo shop bathroom...

"Hey... Yeah, mom.. No, I didn't get arrested again... No, I'm fine... No, my boyfriend is not in trouble. No, he did not break my heart. I am. Yes, I am out of mac and cheese. How'd you know?... I love how you always know. Anyways, I think I found my real twin, so like, can he be in the fam or what?" She asks, clearly getting off course, then steering herself back. She smiles. "Great! Here he is!"

She hands Parker the phone.

"New mom?" He asks hesitantly. He smiles and waddles outside to talk.

I hiss in pain, but then it stops. "All done," Bobby says. He gets a mirror and shows me. I smile.

"It's great! Thanks!" I say, sitting up but then yelping as it hurts. Sam steadies me before releasing me. Laney lays sideways on the table, and he begins on her. She yelps like I did, and Sam doesn't look too good about it.

The Laila and Giana chick were both talking about annoying things their boyfriends do.

"Where's Kehlani and Ryder?" Sam asks. I point at the bathroom, where a single smack sound is heard from there just after I point, perfect timing. He shudders in disgust.

"YOU'RE SUCH A DOUCHE!" I hear Kehlani screech. Was she slapping him? Sam storms over to the door, banging on it three times when he gets there.

"Who's a douche?! What are you doing to my sister, Ryder?!" Sam yells, banging on the door some more. Laney hisses in pain, and he glances over to make sure she's okay before his gaze goes back to the door. It opens, and Kehlani comes out with a bunch of soap all over the top of her chest, above her cleavage. Ryder laughs behind her, holding up a soapy hand.

"You take everything too seriously," Kehlani says, walking out with a paper towel now in hand, wiping herself off.

"Can't help it is. Used to protecting you." Sam admits sheepishly. She smiles as she throws the paper away.

"Think you wouldn't be with the basically three years being away from each other." She says, smiling up at him. His eyes flash with anger. She must have a good story on her.

"Riot locations?" Liv asks, reminding us. Parker steps in with a giant smile on his face, a blush slightly on his cheeks, making him look adorable as he hands her her phone back.

"There's a Walmart with a rodents issue in the girl's bathroom right down the road." I inform her.

Liv smiles. "Perfect. It was nice meeting you all. Byyyeee! Lai! GiGi!" She says. They look up and sigh as they follow her out, waving to us. They may seem irritated, but I'm willing to bet she's really fun.

After about an hour of talking and throwing chips at each other, Laney is done. We all watch as Kehlani shamelessly just kind of takes off her shirt and lays down on the table. Bobby smiles to himself.

"No fucks given." Bobby states, and we all laugh but Ryder and Sam, who don't look pleased.

It takes a few hours for hers, considering she had to get hers removed. Her face shows no pain whatsoever, she just lays there, yawning every so often.

"Are you sure it doesn't hurt?" Ryder asks nervously. I smile at his care for her.

"Mm. Nah. Felt worse in any case." She mumbles. Anger flashes in his eyes.

"If you don't mind me asking, how'd you get the scar?" I ask curiously. She smiles, her eyes closed.

"I was shot." She says. Laney, Sam, and Ryder all look angry. Touchy subject I'm guessing...? I nod in understanding, curious, but keeping to myself. Kehlani seems like a mystery. You can't help but want to know more.

Suddenly, the door opens again, and three guys peek their heads in.

"Quick question, where are our girlfriends?" One with blonde hair asks.

"Walmart down the road, Liv's starting a riot." Kehlani states, showing no struggle with the pain being caused on her back.

"Jesus." They all say and shut the door, and we see them start running down the road, where cop lights are seen. Oh my.

Later on, hours later when Kehlani and Ryder had gone home, Sam and Laney were passed out on the couch, me and Parker were talking on the balcony.

"What's next?" I ask with a smile, looking over the city which has become so bright to me. Never was before. Wonder why.

"Anything you want, Flower. Anything you want."

"I'm thinking... Number 14."

"Well, then, lets shoot for the stars."

"How do you shoot for the stars by jumping off of a cliff?" I ask him, confused, which leads to him showing me an article about a girl who'd committed suicide by jumping off of a cliff not too recently, and how she had said she'd wanted to be with the stars to her friends and lover.

Oh my.

How does he find this stuff?

"That isn't funny, Parker."

You know what... I'm going to quit asking...

It's Parker West, after all.

Chapter 9

"Uh.. Question..." Parker trails off, jogging up to me with the rest of the team behind him.

"Yeah?" I question.

"Can we get out early today? We have plans after practice and I blew off two parties for this." He says as if exasperated.

"I didn't ask you to blow off those parties, now did I? I have a treat for you boys for working so hard though." I tell them with a smile.

My brother pulled a few strings.

I lead them all out to the back of the building, where a huge new building waits.

"What's this?" Leroy asks.

"Go in." I tell them. They all excitedly run towards it, and Parker throws the doors open, and they all yell in excitement before charging, ripping off their shirts and taking off their shoes and socks before jumping into the pool. "Now, its not only for you guys, its donated to the entire school, so don't be all: 'this is our mancave, get out', because that is not fair."

I tell them. Parker, dripping wet, comes creeping into my line of sight, and pulls me in for a hug.

He pulls back, his eyes suddenly lit up. He grabs my bag from my shoulder and pulls out my bluetooth speaker and my phone. He hooks it up before going to YouTube.

What comes out of the speakers makes me contemplate suicide for the third time in my life.

Its out with the old, and in with the new. Goodbye clouds of grey, hello skies of blue.

I put a hand over my face, and Parker starts dancing like twins wearing purple in Charlie Brown. I cringe.

A dip in the pool, a trip to the spa. Endless days in my shades. The whole world according to moi!

Parker starts to do.. I don't know how to describe it. He puts his hands in the air and shakes.. No.. Rolls his hips in different directions as if he were a girl grinding on a male in a club.

Iced tea imported from England. Lifeguards imported from Spain. Towels, imported from Turkey. Turkey imported from Maine.

We're gonna relax and renew.

You go do!

Parker grabs my purse as the last line goes and takes out my hair brush.

He starts to runway walk down the isle, swaying his hips dramatically.

I want FABULOUS! That is my simple request. All things FABULOUS! Bigger and better the best. I need something inspiring to help me get along.

I need fabulous, is that so wrong?

Parker turns around dramatically at that last word, and slips on stray water, tumbling into the pool but not after hitting his head on the side. After making sure he wasn't unconscious, I pause the song and burst out laughing.

"Stop laughing every time I fall!" Parker whines, causing me to smack the nearby table with my fist, laughing harder before dramatically putting up my knee and slapping it.

Bad move.

He grabs my lower leg and yanks me forcefully into the pool.

I smile to myself, the plan already forming.

I start thrashing around, and he clearly can't tell I'm serious because he's too busy laughing.

I give up and slowly sink to the bottom of the pool. Just to make a show out of it, I release some air so bubbles come up.

"SHIT!" I hear several voices scream above before about five guys dive after me. Parker is the first to make it. I shut my eyes and pretend to be asleep. I feel my body get pulled from the water, and placed on the cool tiles. I let my body fall limp, and let some water dribble from my mouth.

"Your such an idiot, Parker!" Someone yells at him.

He shakes my shoulders, but I keep up the act. Suddenly, my stomach is being pushed on twice. I open my eyes just quickly enough to see his face collide with mine, his lips roughly pressing against mine to blow air into my mouth.

Well.

Well..

Well...

Damn.

His lips, soft, with a bit of edge from being cracked, just perfect, fitting nicely against mine. I wont deny the series of fireworks exploding throughout my entire being, but after all, this is kind of like a first kiss anyways?

There's no way you can catch feelings that quickly.

Can you?

I realize he's still blowing air into me, and shove him off, screeching slightly.

It happened in all but three seconds, but it felt like a lifetime.

"You're okay!" He says, pulling me to his chest. I feel his heartbeat. Its so fast. "Oh god. I thought I killed you. I thought.. I thought I lost you." He breathes.

"Dude I was acting." I squeak.

"I don't care. God that was so scary."

Is he as afraid to lose me as I am him?

"You... You... You...... You... You NEANDERTHAL!" I scream out. "DO YOU KNOW WHAT THIS MEANS?!" I scream, pushing him away from me.

His friends go back to splashing each other, but I notice them glancing over, clearly listening.

"What?" He asks.

"Number 5 on the list, Parker!" I hiss at him quietly so the other's can't hear. His eyes widen.

"At least it wasn't with a stranger?"

"Fuck. Off. Parker. You. Fuck.Ing. Id. I. Ot." I speak the syllables as if they were separate words entirely.

"Use your wo.rd.sss." He says sarcastically. I smack him upside the head before grabbing a towel and my stuff and stomping out.

I don't deny the smile as I burst out the doors.

We're currently walking around Walmart, Jordan in the stroller strapped in because he learned how to fly, and I made some improvements so he shouldn't be able to get out. We're looking for some little human baby spoons. I'm pushing the stroller, Parker's holding the basket.

"WOMEN DON'T DESERVE RIGHTS!" Parker suddenly screams out, making me drop the baby spoons I'd bent over to grab.

"FUCK OFF DOUCHEBAG!" A random voice comes from somewhere in the store. I smile and grab some more of the spoons and putting them in the basket.

"You really need to stop doing that."

"WE SHOULD GET ALL GENDER BATHROOMS!" He yells out, and I shake my head before grabbing some of the banana baby food just because I enjoy eating those myself, and because I made Jordan eat it once and he ate it really quickly, so I assume he likes it. Don't worry, I checked the ingredients, its fine.

"YEAH!" Someone yells out.

"Parker shut up before you get us kicked out." I hiss at him. He looks at the floor. I put the stuff in the basket and push the stroller. I peek underneath the little shade I have down to see Jordan looking up at me. He squawks. I smile and shut it. I love life as of the moment.

"Fine, fine." He mutters. I grab some more ducky bibs and throw those in because Jordan chewed up the one I got him in the beginning, and I lead Parker to the check-out lane. He puts the stuff up.

"Awww. Young couple goals, thank the lord you guys are doing it together." The sixteen year old looking girl named Mindy checking us out says with a hand over her heart. Parker and I just smile. That's all we've gotten from people since we got Jordan, so we just started not denying it. It gets tedious.

I like the ring to it.

Ally West..

Shut up subconscious! We aren't allowed to think that way!

"Do you mind if I see the baby?" Mindy asks. I smile and turn the stroller towards her before lifting it. Her eyes widen. "That's a...." She grabs her phone, and I hear the recording button go off. Oh well.

"Yeah. This is Jordan, our adopted pet duck. We saved his life from a rabid, cruel, harmful seagull." I tell her. "We agreed that I get the duck on weekdays since I have more free time, and I can take care of him other than the ducky-day-care he goes to - totally kidding the duck does go to a sitters when I have class though - and he gets the duck on Friday mornings to Sunday evening." I let her know.

"Why did you decide to keep him?" She asks, smiling, clearly amused.

"I couldn't bare to give him to the ASPCA and have him killed. And I don't know where his flock is, so we filled out papers for both of our apartment buildings and adoption papers, and well, yeah." I finish.

"You guys are amazing. I'm posting this everywhere." She says. The recording ending sound goes off. "Also.. Bill is on me." She says, taking out a shiny platinum card and swiping it through before I can deny.

"Thanks." Parker says, grabbing the bags. I put down the shade thing, and as we walk away, I notice the girl grab a coworker aside and start telling the person. The person laughs.

"I feel happy." I state randomly, a lingering smile on my face.

"You too? Good to know."

Later on, me and Parker are lying on his bed opposite of each other, staring at the ceiling which has a Power Puff Girls poster. His wall also holds posters such as:

Power Rangers, Teen Titans Go!, Girl Meets World, Selena Gomez and The Scene, Dove Cameron, Descendants, 13 Reasons Why, Stranger Things, Mean Girls, A random Disney World resort poster.

Wonder Pets, BackyardagansWow Wow Wubsie and, Teletubies; You heard me right. A Teletubies poster.

I have never been more fucking terrified in my life then the second I laid eyes on that black and white Teletubies poster. Like, what the hell?! Why?!

"Why the random disney resort poster?" I ask curiously. Its just a poster of the park.

"My - uh - my dad promised me he'd bring me when he was little.. He uh... He committed suicide after my mom died of colon cancer." He murmurs quietly. I instantly turn and hug him. He puts one arm around me in response.

"My mom died giving birth to me. My dad abandoned us. Never knew them." I mutter, letting him know that I understand his pain.

"I'm sorry." We both say, even though we both know it won't help anything. Never does.

We both give one single breathed laugh. I sit up and look at him.

"I promise you, I'm bringing you to Disney World, okay?" I offer. His eyes flash with emotion.

"Don't make me promises, please. It always ends up bad for me when someone does."

"Not this time. I promise."

"You know, Ally, you don't cut yourself enough credit." He states with a pondering voice.

"What?" I ask, confused.

"Your actually really cool."

And with that, he turns over and falls asleep. I put a blanket over him and put Jordan in the stroller. Tis Monday.

I smile as I walk home.

You too, Parker. You too.

Chapter 10

"Hey. You disappeared last night." Parker says when I answer the phone. I sigh, putting a hand to my head.

"You're acting like we hooked up only your the girl for once." I tell him. He laughs quietly.

"Ha yeah whatever, I got plans for us though... We can do it after school. Do you mind if I take Jordan for the day?" He asks curiously.

"Sure. Hurry up and get over here though. I need to get to school." I tell him. He soon swings by and grabs Jordan, and then leaves again. As I walk into class, eyes are on me, and I don't know why. I sit in my normal seat, and soon a girl comes up and asks where I got my shirt from. I'm confused.

Then my third class... Something... Strange.......

A random guy. He sits beside me, leaning on his desk and looking at me with a side-ways smile.

"Hey." He says with a smooth voice.

"Uh.. Hi.." I say awkwardly, scooting away from him. He takes it upon himself to scooch closer.

"Do you need something? Confused on a question..?" I trail off questioningly. He smiles. He grabs a strand of hair and twirls it in his fingers.

"Can't just come over and talk to a pretty girl?" He asks. I swallow, kind of scared that he's going to try what Braden did, and move away from him.

"Not when it's me buddy." I mumble. I see movement in the door's window. I look to see Parker running towards the door with a bundle in his hands. I start crawling over the seats to get there quickly. He bursts the door open.

"It's Jordan!" He yells out frantically.

"What did you do?!" I ask quickly, taking him from him. I open it to see Jordan perfectly fine.

"He got a cut on his back." He says nervously. I check and see a tiny, tiny, tiny scratch.

"Really." I deadpan. "You interrupted my learning and observation of the male species known as 'jocks' to tell me our child only has this tiny scratch?" I ask.

"Wait, you guys have a kid?!" Some girl screeches and runs forward. When she sees Jordan, and he sees her, he quacks loudly, causing her to scream and jump back.

Good thing the teacher isn't in here...

People are suddenly surrounding us, getting a peek at Jordan and 'aww'ing.

"Parker, you need to realize I'm not always free. You have part-time custody and that means that you have responsibility to create with Jordan. I'm not always going to just be here to help all the time, you know." I reprimand him.

He looks sad. He covers it quickly, though.

"I know." He mutters. "I just missed having you around." He mumbles quietly. I glance around, ignoring the glares I'm receiving because he said that. I give him Jordan before grabbing my stuff and slinging my backpack on, dragging him out by the arm.

"The good girl ditching class? Woooow!" He says as if truly shocked.

"Shut up, moron. What did you have planned?"

He smiles devilishly.

Oh no.

"Parker, where are we?" I ask.

"My dealer's place."

"WHAT?!" I screech. He laughs freely.

"Weed, Ally, Weed. Calm down." He says, laughing again. "God I love the innocence in you." He says. My heart skips a beat for a second.

"Parker... You're going really quick with this list thing." I squeak. He laughs.

"Its just one blunt, and one cigarette. You don't even have to smoke the whole things. Just one puff of each. Alright?" He asks. I bite my lip, wringing my fingers together for a second before I nod once. He pulls me in. "HEY JOHNNY!" He yells out.

"P-man!" The person replies.

"This here, is my girl Ally, who has never smoked a day in her life and its on her bucket list. Hook us up?"

God, how I love when he says 'my girl'.

"Yooou got it!" The guy says before going ahead and getting whatever. Parker pays and shoves it in his pocket before dragging me out. We get to my apartment and he sits me at the kitchen counter. He rolls up a blunt and pulls out a lighter. He puts a pack of cigarettes on the counter.

I quickly grab Jordan where he is in his stroller and put him in his crib that now has a net on top so he can't fly away, putting his food and a little water bowl in.

I rush back to the kitchen and sit.

"Go ahead." He says. I slowly grab a cigarette, and put it in my mouth. I lean forward so he can light it.

Just as he lights it, Laney walks in and stops instantly when she sees us.

"What the fuck are you doing to Ally?" She asks, her voice slightly angered now. "I said get out more, not start smoking and doing drugs, Ally. I thought you were a good influence." She says to Parker at the end. I pull a drag and start coughing.

"EW!" I sputter out. "Jesus. Melinda smoked one every day. Eck. How did she do that?" I ask myself as I put it out.

"Who's Melinda?" Parker asks.

"I guess I should tell you both.. I don't really want to.... Laney I'm only smoking because of my... Bucket list." I tell her. Her face smooths out.

"Ooooh. Okay. All good then." she says and walks out. "Also," she says, peeking her head back, "save some of the blunt for me." She walks away after that. I smile and laugh once before putting the blunt on my lips. He lights it. I take a drag, and instantly yank it out of my mouth and put it out. I cough hard. He laughs as he pats my back. Once I calm down, he smokes some of the blunt.

I try a couple more times, and it gets better once I know my limit.

After a while, the urge to eat surges in me. I've never been one to eat, really. Always had a small appetite. But right now, I want to eat. I hop down and waddle to the cabinets before throwing it open. He puts out the blunt and joins me. We eat chips together, occasionally throwing chips at each other's faces and laughing.

Suddenly, he takes the dip container and smashes it on my face. My eyes are shut, my mouth open in a wide 'o'. He roars with laughter as he sets the container on the counter and rinses off his hand. I sit there, gaping. Suddenly, shocking him, I tackle him to the ground and rub my cheek against his cheek. He yells out to stop, so I rub my face all over his shirt.

"Noooo! Not my Britney Spears shirt!"

"God, your worse than Shane Dawson!"

(A/N: please note this was written years before Shane Dawson got cancelled. I am no longer a fan or supporter.)

"I wish I was Shane Dawson. He gets paid to do what he loves." He says with an envious tone.

"So do you." I say, slightly confused.

"Stop making points!" He whines. I shake my head before walking off, heading for a shower.

We had been called in to get a tag on Jordan's leg so if he ever got lost, they'd know where to return him to by the address thingy on there.

Now, we were currently walking through the park, Jordan all strapped up.

"HEY!" a female voice calls out suddenly. We both turn to see those two teenage girls that looked 16 from when Parker fell and tripped me, and they called us 'couple goals'. They were surrounded by a few more girls. "Its fall-boy and trip-girl!"

"Shark boy and lava girl would have worked too." Parker mutters under his breath as they all come forward. I giggle quietly.

"Aww, did you guys adopt?" One girl squeals.

"In a way." I say with a smile. Parker lifts the veil and reveals the duck who on perfect timing honks. They all jump, and start giggling like schoolgirls as they pet him.

"You guys are the cutest couple I have ever seen." One girl says with a bright smile. We both smile.

Soon enough, we're out of that lil' situation and walking along.

"You already decided what we're doing next, didn't you?" I ask Parker, carefully moving around a pot-hole. He smiles a bright, crooked, dimple-flashing, panty-dropping smile in my direction, looking at me.

Of course he fails to see a pot hole in front of him.

Of course, I say nothing.

And he eats shit, falling to the ground.

He groans in pain, rubbing at his leg.

"You're such an idiot." I tell him truthfully. He laughs under his breath, not even bothering to deny it.

"Yes, I've already decided what we're doing this weekend." He informs me, dropping the hint that its this weekend.

"Only you."

"Only me indeed."

Chapter 11

W ell, Friday rolled around, and as I got back from my walk with Jordan, there sat one car belonging to one Parker West and he comes out of my apartment with a suitcase that happens to be mine.

"Give Jordan to Laney, and get in." Is all he says.

Well, its Parker, so I decide to trust him - for once - and do as he says. When he pulls out, I take a glance back at the stuff in the back. "Where...? What..?" I trail off.

"We're going camping!"

I bang my head back.

Oh no.

"What are you doing?!"

"I don't know!" I wail out, flailing my arms.

"Well stop standing there jumping around like a 17 year old anime girl who's falling in love with her demon protector that helps her with her shrine and get to fixing it!" Parker reprimands me.

Does he watch Kamisama Kiss or what?

"No I do not!" He hisses, his face turning red.

Oops, did I ask that out loud?

"YES YOU DID!" He yells at me. "And don't judge Kamisama Kiss! That's the best anime ever!" He hisses at me, and I fall into laughter.

"D-dude! You've got it wrong! Your Lie In April is the best." I tell him, giggling again at the end.

"No, you've got it wrong. Obviously its a tie between Cory In The House and Darude Sandstorm."

And there goes my lungs because I basically roar with laughter, and it echos on the trees around us.

"Come on, lets take a walk." Parker says, taking the bug spray away from me before spraying me down correctly. He grabs my wrist and starts to lead me somewhere. Slowly, he lets go. We find ourselves on a rocky road.

"I already don't want to go back." He says with a sheepish smile.

"I'm not sure about it yet." I say, laughing slightly.

"Everything is fine until you come back." He mutters, kicking a rock.

"Some people never get to come back." I whisper. He looks over at me before stopping, grabbing my shoulders and turning me to him.

"What do you mean." He demands instantly. Fear builds in my chest. His eyes search my face when I don't answer. "What do you mean, Ally? Sometimes you say things.. really fucked up things, out of nowhere and your face... you get this expression like you're not even here. It terrifies me." He says, his voice coming out afraid. His hands find their way to my arms and he holds my wrists to his face.

"You won't find them there." I whisper, tears building in my eyes. I didn't want him to know. Anything.

"But I'll find them somewhere?" He asks, his face breaking. I look at the ground. I grab his wrist and make him help me onto a nearby huge rock. I move my legs so he can see the inside of my thighs, always hidden. He grabs my thighs and puts his head close so he can see the old-ish scars.

My heart decides to freak out, my thoughts running a lil bit wild.

"They're old." I tell him quietly. "I didn't.."

He moves quickly before me, his hands coming to either side of my waist, our chests just touching as a flash of anger crosses his expression.

"You didn't want to tell me. Why do you actually have that bucket list, Ally, because if getting it done is steps closer to you committing suicide, or something, then I'm out."

Fear like no other entrances my body, and I instantly wrap my arms around his neck and lock my thighs around his torso.

"Don't leave me. Please. Please, don't leave me." I whisper in a broken voice into the depth of his neck. His arms wrap around my waist.

"I need you to talk to me, Ally, please. Why do you have that bucket list?" He asks lowly.

"M-my best friend killed herself two years ago." I whisper, finally admitting the cold truth. His body freezes. "I didn't... I didn't see it like you just did. I knew she was sad that her ex cheated on her but I didn't know... Its all my fault." I sob into his neck, tears falling rapidly. "D-don't leave me." I cry out.

"I'm not. I'm never going to leave you, Ally. Not now, not ever. It isn't your fault. Suicide is an option for depressed people to take the easy way out. It's not your fault. It was nobody's fault. She did it on her own." He says in a sad voice. I can hear the pity. But I don't want it. I don't want his pity.

His next question makes me slightly freeze up. "How old are they?"

No response.

"Ally. Fucking tell me!" He sharply demands, leaning back to look me in the eyes.

"A-almost a m-month."

His body shivers, with what I assume is disgust.

"Can... Can you just tell me why you stopped?" He murmurs, questioningly.

"You." I whisper. His eyes widen, but his lips tug, like he'd gotten the answer he wanted. "I.. I knew you'd be disappointed, or disgusted, like you are now."

"I'm not disgusted, Ally, I'm sad. Who.. Who found her?" He asks. I shut my eyes, tilting my head down as the images soar through my brain in the speed of a hummingbird's wings.

"..I did."

That's all it takes for him to pull me to him, crushing me in the warmest of hugs.

"This is too sad. I feel overwhelmed. Can we do something, talk about something else?" I ask.

"Yeah, come on, lets go start a campfire."

"Its so pretty." I whisper, my subconscious taking note on how our thighs brush each other's every time we move.

"Yeah. I always liked to think it as dancing, the flames, to an unknown tune, or maybe they're making their own music, living as great as possible for the time being because their lives are so short." He murmurs, his hand slightly moving over on his leg in my direction.

I grab my phone.

"Lets give them music. The dancing flame provides us warmth, a way to cook, a way to boil water if ever needed, beauty, light... Let's give back." I say, looking at him in the lights from the fire.

"I'm game."

PARKER's POV

She looks so beautiful in the firelight.

Her dark hair, even darker. Her blue eyes shine brighter. Her cheekbones can be seen more prominent with the shading, and her feminine jawline is creating shadows down the edges of her neck, disappearing as her shirt comes to view.

Does she at all notice my staring?

I doubt it.

But how could she not? It's all I do.

"I'm game." I tell her. She smiles and hands me her unlocked phone. I go to YouTube and search my desired song, finding it fitting.

I hear the drums echoing tonight, but she hears only whispers of some quiet conversation...

She's coming in twelve-thirty flight, her moonlit wings reflect the stars that guide me towards salvation.

She smiles and grabs my wrist before starting a slow dance with me. She's become more bold. I love that about being with her. I want to keep drawing this side of her out, keep watching as she starts to shine brighter and brighter.

I stopped an old man along the way, hoping to find some long forgotten words or ancient melodies. He turned to me as if to say, "hurry boy its waiting there for you!"

Its gonna take a lot to drag me away from you. There's nothing that a hundred men or more could ever do. I bless the rains down in africa.. Gonna take some time to do the things we never had.

The wild dogs cry out in the night, as they grow restless, longing for some solitary company. I know what I must do what's right. As sure as Kilimanjaro rises like Olympus above the Serengeti.

I seek to cure what's deep inside, frightened of this thing that I've become.

Its gonna take a lot to drag me away from you, there's nothing that a hundred more could ever do. I bless the rains down in africa. Gonna take some time to do the things we never had.

Hurry boy, she's waiting there for you.

Its gonna take a lot to drag me away from you. There's nothing that a hundred men or more could ever do. I bless the rains down in africa. I bless the rains down in africa. I bless the rains down in africa. I bless the rains down in Africa. I bless the rains down in africa.

Gonna take some time to do the things we never had...

She stops before releasing me and clapping in excitement.

When we're done, and she's asleep in the bed beside me, I subtly scoot closer to her. She's so warm.

Did she...

Could she...

Could she feel my heart beat flying?

Chapter 12

"Truth or dare."

"Truth," I replied easily.

"Why have you never liked... Uh. Had. You know... Um... Why have you never like, smashed with anyone?" He blurts out quickly. I laugh freely.

"1. I'm ugly. 2. I was even uglier in high school. 3. I wanted to wait for someone that I fully heatedly loved. Genuinely. I've never really given myself the opportunity. Every time a guy would try with me, I'd push away. You're the first male I've like, ever spoken to aside from my brother and Raider." I state, looking up at the clouds above us.

"Raider?"

"Childhood best friend. Haven't seen him since freshman year. We still talk a few times a week, but I haven't seen him face to face in forever."

"Bitch better square up. Your mine." He says, looking at the clouds as well. My eyes widen very slightly at his words. Is it wrong to like that? Being called his? No. Yes. Yes, it is wrong.

"Calm down, Parker," I mutter. "Your like, my only friend. Laney is my roommate Hendrik is just kind of an acquaintance."

"I don't care. I should get a sign and put it on you somewhere, reading: 'Property of Parker West, if found, return immediately.' Yeah.. yeah I like that." He thinks to himself. A smile grows over my face.

"You're so stupid." I breathe. He smiles.

And we just lay there, the sound of our breathing, the birds chirping, crickets sounding, trees creaking as they move with the slight wind. The trees were a magnificent green as of the moment.

For the shortest of time, I felt infinite.

"Let's go hiking." Parker randomly offers.

"Let's go hiking up to a mountain and jump off the cliff into like, water," I say. He smiles and gets up. He brushes his jeans before and helps me up. I brush mine off before we start getting what we need, according to him. Parker knows everything, I swear. Well, almost.

We change and then start walking, and a smile grows over my face as I inspect the beauty of the trees around us, sunlight peeking through, stunning me.

Eventually, we get to the clearing.

Something confuses me about it.

Off to the side, the wayside, there looks to be a sign or a shrine...?

I start walking to it.

In memory of Winter Star.

"Parker?" I call out.

"Yeah?" He asks.

"I don't think jumping here is safe. Someone died here." I tell him. His eyes widen.

"Ooooh. We're at Suicide Side. No, if we go to the left side it's safe. There are no rocks or anything over there. This spot over here is dangerous." He tells me. I nod and he leads me away from the shrine. Once we get to where he says it's safe, I take off my shirt and shorts.

He does the same.

CHIIIILLLL.

Remember I said we changed? God.

I have an aqua bikini on, and he has black trunks on. He looks me up and down a few times. "That color looks good on you." He says, still looking.

"My eyes are up here," I say, slightly cringing. He smiles and gives me one last once-over before simply jumping. I watch him yell out in excitement before he splashes into the water. When he surfaces, he whoops.

"Come on, Flower!" He yells up at me.

"Uh... I don't know.."

"Do you want to live or not?"

For some reason, when he says that, I hear Melinda's voice as well as his as if she were standing beside me.

I jump.

Adrenaline even better than ever soars through my body, taking flight like an eagle in the wind. I surface and smile at him, slightly shivering from how cold the water is. "Was that great or what?!" He asks, swimming over and pulling me in for a hug. I laugh into his chest.

"Yeah... Yeah, that was pretty great."

We were now back at the campsite, me lying down on the table while Parker 'properly takes care of my scars' for me.

"Why are you so afraid that I'm going to leave?" Parker asks quietly. My heartbeat is freaking out as I feel his breath on my leg as he continues to put whatever ointment he has on them. My leg slightly twitches.

"I don't like talking about myself," I whisper.

"Ally, I want to know about you, so I can stay."

God dammit.

"My mother died giving birth to me, my father left because he blamed me, Melinda... Parker everyone always winds up leaving me." I whisper.

"Ally, I'm not going to leave you."

"You say that now, but look at the facts, Parker. It's a list. A list, so you have amusement, a list so I can do all these things... But then what's next? What happens after the list is over? Done? Completed? There's going to be nothing to keep you here, to keep you amused."

"Ally. Whatever you think is what you think." He says. I sit up and face him. He holds a sad smile. "I'm still going to be here, no matter what. Think about days when we aren't doing a list thing. We chill out and still have fun. It'll be like that." He points out.

"You'll get bored eventually," I say with a laugh. "Guys like you always do."

"Guys... Like me?" He asks. He looks angry now. "Ally, what exactly do you mean?"

"I mean that guys like you get bored of the same thing! You're always going to parties, Parker, I've seen the Facebook posts. You do crazy things like go skydiving, hook up, or just have genuine fun. Parker, you're always doing something different whether or not you choose to believe it, or see it."

He looks genuinely shocked.

"I don't want that anymore." He says.

"You don't want what?"

"I don't want parties and skydiving and hooking up. Not anymore. I really don't want it." He tells me, leaving me shocked.

"Then what do you want?" I ask before I can stop myself.

"....You."

Chapter 13

"Here's your latte!" The nice barista says, and I thank her before going over to my typical corner seat. Parker was on his way with Jordan.

"OH. EM. GEE. Ally?!" A familiar voice calls out. I look up from my laptop to see a man in a fluorescent pink tank top, blue leggings, and Converse sneakers. I raise an eyebrow. He squeals. "Girl, it's been forever!" He says, grabbing my arm, and pulling me up from the chair, and into his arms.

"Gee, Ally, the way you're always around Parker, you'd think you're a one-woman type of girl!" Someone calls out. I roll my eyes. The strange, exotic yet intriguing man pulls away and faces the jock.

"Uhm, I'm gay, if you couldn't tell. Ew." The man says, shutting his eyes for a second before opening them wide, raising his eyebrows the same way Shane Dawson does in his videos sometimes. "Also, shut up you low-life, sexy, greek god-like worthless hottie. No one messes with my Mint."

Mint.

The name brings up childhood memories, and I finally piece it together.

"Hendrik?!"

"Took you long enough bitch! Oh my god, we have to catch up. Ooh! Ooh! Manni Peddie's like the ones your brother used to pay for us when he started modeling! By the way, your brother now, DAYUM."

"I'm highly uncomfortable," I say, laughing, but pulling him in for another hug. "My god. It's great to see you again! And yes, definitely. This time on me."

"You work? Where, when, how, why?"

This dude knows me.

"Really?" I give him a dumbfounded look. "Look at my brother. A wicked huge model. And you think I wouldn't now and then pick up an odd job with these connections...?"

"Oh my fucking god you've MODELED?!"

"Of course, queen."

"YES, my main ho! Yes! I've always dreamed of this!" He exclaims, jumping once and clapping. I sit him down. "Where and when have you modeled?!" He asks.

"Only a couple of times. Once in Paris. One time in Turkey. One time in Switzerland. Uh... Dubai.. and London. Makes good pay and I don't try too hard. I don't even understand. I was ugly throughout high school and middle, and elementary, and birth.." I trail off, self-loathing.

"Bitch, it's called a glow-up. Puberty's final step hit you like a top of bricks sweetheart... Wait... You don't do that thing where you wear sweaters and boyfriend jeans all the time, right? Wait. That's what you're wearing right now, oh god, Ally!" He exclaims.

"Wait... Why are you here?" I ask curiously.

"I just transferred schools to Wilston." He says, smiling.

"No shit, that's where I go."

"Yes. Bitch. Anyways, I'm here now and I'm going to get you out of this... Getup." He says, pulling his bag off of his shoulder. "Oh my god, you are so lucky my sister just gave me this stuff to give to my friend Vanessa. Well, fake friend. I hate that bitch."

I'm confused.

He pulls out a black dress that would be around two inches above my knees and hands it to me. I raise an eyebrow. He pulls out his heels.

He then studies my features.

"This won't do at all. Come in the bathroom with me so we can do your makeup. And those eyebrows. Jesus, Al." He mutters. I pout in offense but follow him, ignoring the wolf whistles. I hear the door open, and people calling out Parker's name. Hendrik grabs my wrist and tugs me in.

I go into the stall and put on the dress and heels. I come out and look in the mirror. I look... Different. I only dress up when on occasion I take a deal. Hendrik squeals and grabs my wrist before tugging me over. He brings out tweezers and instantly starts going at it without warning. I stay still and silent. When done, he does my eyeliner winged, puts on mascara - while commenting that I don't need false lashes because mine are already long as hell sentences - and lightly puts on a lipstick.

"I don't look the same," I state, looking in the mirror as he puts my clothes in his bag, along with his makeup.

We walk out, to see Parker standing above a group of jocks, looking pissed as hell, his hands in fists, his jaw clenched.

"Don't talk about her that way." He says in a low tone. Hot.

"Just layin' out the facts P. She went into the bathroom with a man who looked quite eager. Looks like your little Ally isn't so innocent after all. I mean, look how she's dressed." The guy, Chuck, says while waving an arm my way. I raise an eyebrow as Parker looks over, his eyes widening, the hard expression leaving his face for a second as his jaw goes slack.

I smirk and approach Chuck, newfound confidence in this dress. I sit on the edge of his knee.

"And you'd know?" I ask him, leaning in. His eyes widen before a cocky expression consumes his face. He rests a hand on my knee.

"Ally, what are you doing?" Parker asks. "What are you wearing?"

"Wanna see something cool? Wanna know a secret?" I ask Chuck. He nods. I look at Hendrik and motion toward my laptop. I close down Word and bring up the online articles about me. "Look it, there I am in an even shorter dress, skin-tight, six-inch heels," I say in an innocent tone. He swallows. His hand raises slightly.

"Ally, what the hell are you doing?" Parker asks, trying to get my attention.

"Oh, that's me and my brother, I'm sure you know him. Big model for Rolex, this one here we're both wearing Rolex watches, him in a suit, me in a dress even shorter." I say with a smirk.

"Ally, what's gotten into you? What are you doing?"

"You know, Chuck, sometimes I get so tired of being me. I pretend to be good. But look, I've even modeled for Victoria's Secret." I say and scroll to the picture of me and a couple of other models lying in a bed, laughing as if we were joking around and having a fun sleepover in our bras and lace panties.

I start to feel a bulge in his pants, and I try hard not to break my stone expression.

"That was shot in Paris. It was a fun weekend. I even brought along a... lover. I do on every trip I go on." I state. The other Jocks are all looking shocked as hell. "Wanna go to Greece with me tomorrow?"

"Is that where you're going? You said you had plans with your brother." Parker states sidetracked for the moment.

"Yeah, baby, I'm down. Especially after seeing that. Why do you hide that Princess?" Chuck asks, raising his hand further.

"So no one can see it. Ever." I state in my normal voice, standing, revealing his bulge. His friends all start laughing. I pretend to dust off my hands. "That's a genuine photo by the way. No, I don't bring lovers on my trips. Parker, you're ticket is already bought though, so maybe there's a first time for everything," I wink suggestively." Hendrik, would you like to come with?"

"Can I bring my boyfriend?"

"Duh."

"It's so stupid. You can't have your pet duckling with you on your trip even when sitting first class? Ugh. I want my baby." Parker whines. I roll my eyes.

"Parker, someone could be allergic," I explain. He huffs, crossing his arms.

"Whatever. I still want my duck." He says. I grab my tiny bag by my foot that I'd hidden, open it, take out the stuffed duck toy, and offer it to him. He smiles and takes it, hugging it fiercely. "Ally, you scared me yesterday."

"What do you mean?" I ask.

"Yesterday when you were fucking with Chuck. I thought you had just gone all dark and something happened while I was gone. I'm worried when you're not near me. I'm rather... we'll I'm rather possessive. I didn't like seeing you dressed like that in front of other men, and I especially didn't appreciate you sitting on his lap."

Swoon.

Wait...

No swooning. We don't swoon, Ally. We're not allowed to swoon!

"It's my inner little demon, Parker. I lost the fucks given. I never really get like that. But I just felt like it. I don't know.." I trail off. He looks over at me.

"Am I a bad influence on you?" He ponders.

I sit up and look down at him with a bewildered expression.

"It's been almost two months since we met and you're just now figuring this out?" I deadpan. How stupid but adorable can he be?

"Hmm." That is all he says.

"Parker, I just got out of work, what is it?"

"Shut up, that was like an hour or two long. Less time because Hendrik already did your makeup... Speaking of... Where is he and his boyfriend?"

"They went back to the hotel," I inform him. He grabs my hand and leads me to the car. A fluttering goes through my stomach.

"So where are we going?" I ask, a smile lifting my features as we get to the car.

"Get in the driver's seat." That is all he demands. I raise my eyebrows but do as he pleases. He gets in the passenger. "I assume you know how to drive."

"Yeah, what I meant in the list was that I've never driven just for fun. It was always to go somewhere that I had to be, or to get something, never just to hit the open roads and drive."

"Well then, let's go."

We wound up in the countryside of Greece, driving for no reason whatsoever, listening to music, laughing, having fun, and living.

Parker West, you truly are something else.

Chapter 14

The day wasn't over yet, Parker still had plans. We had driven back into the main parts of the area in Athens, the city we were currently residing in.

"I want to live here someday. I love Greece." I tell Parker with a smile. He returns it and looks back out the window.

"STOP THE CAR!" He yells at me. I screech to a stop and pull over. We get out and he pulls me towards his destination - a fortune teller. I sigh to myself as we walk in.

"Hello, troubled souls." That is all the creepy lady at the desk says. "You have come for amusement," she says, looking at Parker. "And you've come because he made you."

"How'd you know?" I query.

"Well aside from the fact that I'm a fortune teller, I saw your car outside come to a sudden halt and the young man drag you in."

"Damn, she's good," Parker says to himself. I roll my eyes at his stupidity.

I'd question why he has such good grades and how he's so good at school, but I'm aware of his photographic memory so that explains it well enough. He goes by what his eyes see, he has book smarts but he truly does not have any common sense whatsoever.

"It's ten to get a reading on what your like right now, twenty for now and a future. As of the moment we have a buy one get one free deal." She informs us.

Kinda fake ass shit is this..?

Parker pulls out a twenty and hands it to her, telling her we'll take the buy one get one free on both things. She smiles and pulls us into a dark room with candles and a crystal ball in the center on the floor, small red pillows to sit on across from one.

"Sit." She commands as she sits on one. We sit across from her. She takes Parker's hands and closes her eyes. She breathes out slowly.

"Relax, and open your mind." She whispers. He lets his shoulders sag.

"Right now in time, you are confused. Part of you wants something, part of you is too scared to get it because you might fail, or lose it."

His eyes widen.

"Your distraught over an accident? Something that happened a long time ago to someone important. You feel compassion, sadness, and the need to make something happy. Good." She states.

He smiles a little at the end.

"In the future, you are going to be upset about something. Soon, you're going to be sad about something. Far in the future, you're going to be happy again, but after you do something bad." She says. She opens her eyes.

"Well, I'm scared." He says. I laugh once and the woman grabs my hands next.

I relax. She closes her eyes, and a wave of emotion washes over her features like sand on the beach.

"There's so much. You wish you'd known your mother. You want to hurt your father. You harbor a deep anger. There are three other people you want to bring harm to. Your so sad." She says softly. Parker turns his head to look at me, so I shut my eyes.

"Not only do you want to bring harm to those three people. You want to bring harm to yourself. You hate almost everything. Few things bring you happiness. One specific thing is like the sun, it makes you so bright again."

Parker.

"You're grateful for this brightness. It makes you see things differently. Your happier now than you were about two months ago." She says. She opens her eyes.

"Now do her future!" Parker says, excited.

She shuts her eyes, and relaxes for one moment, just to open them again very wide.

"Oh, my God." She breathes. Her body shakes.

What the hell is she trying to pull on me?

"What?" Parker asks, sounding and looking worried. The woman looks at my hands.

"I cannot bear to say what I have just seen. A little ways away, you're going to have to make a big decision. Between something that brought you overwhelming pain, and something that brought you peace and happiness for a time being. G-good luck." She says.

She releases my hands and walks into a closet to the side, where I hear sobs start. Parker winds an arm around my waist and pulls me out.

I'm confused.

What did she see? What did I do? What do I have to choose? Pain, maybe my dad, Peace, maybe Parker?

I don't want my dad in my life anymore...

I'd choose Parker over my dad any day.

"Don't think about it. It's probably all fake." Parker says, his voice sounding scared.

But then why was it so accurate?

"Girl. That is deep." Hendrik says after I tell him about what happened. "I have a question.."

"Shoot."

"Are you scared of showing Parker who you truly are?" He asks. Parker is currently out buying Greece wine and snacks we can bring home to Jordan tomorrow.

"Yes," I whisper in response.

"The greatest risk any of us will take is to be seen as we are." He tells me quietly. "Show him."

"You did not just quote Cinderella Cinderella," I state, and break into laughter. "Hendrik I'm not a princess, and Parker isn't a prince. We're just two friends."

"No honey, your a queen. And he can be your king so what are you doing sitting around here for, and not out enjoying every moment with him?"

"There's no way any person can catch feelings after only two months, Hen." I laugh, rolling my eyes. He raises his eyebrows.

"Honey," he starts standing up, "don't think I miss the way you two look at each other. Ally, it's possible to fall in love in just two days, let alone two months. Maybe you need to think."

And with that, he leaves me alone to think.

"Can I be un-blindfolded yet?" I ask Parker curiously. He hums with laughter.

"Yes." He replies, and finally takes it off, revealing the roller skating rink.

"All of that for this?" I ask with a blank tone. He laughs and tugs me along. "We're bound to break each other's necks."

He pays us in and gets us skates before helping me up. I wobbly grasp his arms, looking at my feet as he smiles down at me while gently helping me move towards the rink where only two people skate.

The movement underneath, on the skates is enough to make me shake, t e r r i f i e d.

"Loosen up," Parker says in my ear, his hot breath tickling my skin, me shivering.

Dammit Ally, control yourself!

He smiles as if satisfied and I let my back ease up.

He moves to my side and threads our fingers together, gently pulling me along. He's a tiny bit ahead of me as he pulls me.

I pull out my phone and record put surroundings before putting the camera on Parker whose face is hidden due to looking ahead, our linked hands showing at the bottom of the screen.

"Parker," I state.

He looks back and smiles, but then trips, bringing me down with him. We both roar with laughter and I stop recording. He helps me over to the wall, where I then upload it to Instagram, Snapchat, and Twitter with the same caption.

Athens, Greece, with the best.. and the emoji of duckling, camels, first aid and A+P

Everyone in school by now knows about Jordan the duckling. The camels, they won't understand. Parker won't either, until tomorrow. First aid stands for the fact that we just fell, an obviously Ally+Parker.

He laughs as he goes and likes the posts.

"Now that you've technically experienced that, wanna go get pizza?" Parker asks.

"Hell yeah."

"I'm not saying that. I'm saying the perfect man doesn't exist-"

A handsome man in front of us turns to us suddenly.

"Hi, I'm Larry." The random guy who seemed to have been eavesdropping introduces randomly. "My mom calls me 'nugget', we have a fantastic relationship. My parents are happily married after 27 years, I love chocolate milk, memes, school, and work, and I treat women with respect, as I'm actually a feminist myself. If I were yours, I'd want to know if you'd like a foot massage or a shoulder rub. I majored in law and English, I'm smart. I'm outgoing, and I know what I want for my future, I'm not an indecisive kind of man."

I look at Parker.

"I stand corrected."

He gets a squint in his eyes.

"Is that what you're into in guys? Perfect?" He flinches slightly when he says the last word. I look at my milkshake and stir it. Larry goes away promptly.

"No. I'm into guys that... hide their feelings, but if they trust you enough, they'll tell you. Someone that isn't perfect. Maybe have a dark side to them that no one sees. I don't know, just yeah. That was kind of stupid. Ha."

He gives me his full attention, slowly smiling.

"No, no, that was cute." He states, and I blush. I hide it with my hair. He brushes the hair aside. "You're blushing." He whispers, his lips twitching with a smile.

"So?" I ask, blushing harder.

"Nothing. Everything." He mumbles, and grabs his milkshake, and sips it with a lingering smile.

Nothing.

Everything.

I'd be lying if I said Parker West hasn't caught my attention.

Chapter 15

P ARKER's POV

"Parker." She whispers.

"Ally."

Her haunting eyes raise and meet mine, and she smiles. "Kiss me." She demands. I don't waste time, and lean down, touching her lips with my own.

Her lips were soft against mine, fitting perfectly like the missing puzzle piece.

Suddenly, her lips begin to freeze.

She jerks away from me, and chains sprout from the ground and wrap around her wrists.

"Parker!" She screams. They start to dig into her skin, blood dripping from her wrists as she screams in pain. Glass-like walls come from nowhere and a glass box is formed around her.

I bang on the glass, screaming her name.

Music starts to play in the background.

"My hands, my heart, why can't I hold on.. it comes and goes in waves, it always does.."

Water starts coming from sheer nothing and starts filling up the box.

It seems Ally gives up when the water reaches her waist, and she falls limp in the box.

"You couldn't save me." She whispers, it sounding as loud as a shout to the void.

"No! Ally!"

I jerk up, sitting up in the bed Ally and I are sharing. Hendrik and his boyfriend share the other one. Ally is sleeping peacefully beside me, facing me.

I reach out carefully and brush her hair out of her face. I lean down and hover my lips over hers before lightly pressing my lips against hers.

I shut my eyes for one second and pretend it's for real.

I lean away and sigh longingly. She tastes like her chapstick and cherries.

I get off the bed and grab my bag. I pull out some clothes and go into the bathroom. After a steaming shower, I put on some khaki joggers and don't bother putting on a shirt. I stare at myself in the mirror. I turn and raise my fist, and punch the wall.

Breathe in, breathe out.

I try my hardest to regain control of my anger.

"Parker?" Her soft voice reaches my ears. I sigh and pull my fist out of the hole in the wall.

I turn slowly to face Ally. Blood trickles down my hand. I lower my gaze to the floor.

"Parker." She breathes out with worry. She approaches quickly and takes my hand. She silently leads me to the tub. I sit at the edge on command while she gets the first aid kit.

She sits on the edge with me and takes my hand. I focus on her features as she cleans my hand and wraps it. When done, she looks up. I continue to stare.

"What are you staring at?" She whispers.

I lean forward and smash my lips to hers, kissing her passionately.

She leaves me shocked when, after two seconds, she kisses back.

The dream was accurate about how her lips would feel on my own. Perfect. Warm. We move our lips slowly against each other's.

Perfect.

ALLY's POV

His lips feel so nice against mine.

I put one arm around his neck, and the other against his bare chest. He picks me up by the waist and sets me on the sink, stands between my legs, and kisses me again and again.

It just feels... Right.

I tilt my head and kiss back just as fiercely. One of his hands guides me closer to him, the other rests on my thigh.

I don't know what this means for us, but at the moment I can't bring myself to care.

His lips leave mine so I can breathe, and he takes the time to kiss my jaw and my neck, and I make small noises at how good this feels.

"YAS QUEEN! GET THAT ASS!"

Count on Hendrik to ruin the moment. Parker stops kissing my neck and pulls his face back, but stays in place. I breathe heavily, my eyes wide open, limp in one of Parker's arms.

They were all right.

It is possible to catch feelings in just two months.

Parker leans back with a smile.

"We should go to the zoo today." He states.

"Already had it planned. We're going to ride camels too."

"You're awesome." He whispers. We stare at each other before we both, at the same time, lean into each other and go for another passion-filled kiss.

My phone goes off.

INSTAGRAM

HENDRIK_LAMAR_WHO TAGGED YOU IN A POST.

What the hell?

HENDRIK_LAMAR_WHO_: exposed. This is Ally and Parker having a make-out session on the sink. Zoomed in, of course, gotta catch the heat.

"HENDRIK!"

"I hate you so much," I whine as I keep getting tagged in the post. Parker, idiot that he is decided to get on his account through Hendrik's phone and post it on his account with a coy smile as I tried jumping for the phone.

I'm not short, 5'9" but Parker is 6'3" and I can't compete with that.

Now, my notifications were blowing up. I was getting tagged in comments, asking if we were a couple now.

It was one - okay like ten - kiss! Only that!

"Based on that kiss, I don't think you hate me at all," Parker replies cheekily. I go to slap his chest with my free hand, but he catches it and kisses my knuckles.

My heart flutters at the motion.

"Don't be mad at me. Please?" He asks softly. I soften and give in, looking back to the road. He chuckles softly.

The sign for the zoo comes into view, and I pull in quickly.

When parked, I hand Parker his VIP pass.

We get out and walk in together. He randomly grabs my hand, and threads his fingers through mine, shocking me, but making my heart freak out.

"Ahhh Miss Ally, and Mr. Parker. Please, this way." The man at the front desk greets us upon seeing our passes. He gives us a quick tour and then lets us wander.

"Ooh look at the pandas!" Parker gushes.

"I like the brown bear over there," I comment.

"Oh my, the seals!" He squeals.

"Ooh, the sharks!" I say, excited.

"Oh my God, see that demonstration over there, look at the husky the cops have!"

"Aw look at the wolves!"

He turns to me. "Why do you like all of the deadly things?" He asks. I smile.

"Because I want to kill you," I say softly, tapping his nose. He stares down at me before leaning in and kissing me shortly, but long enough to leave me dismantled. He pulls me to the camel section, where our guide waits with a smile. The camels have saddles on. They lead us in with people to help.

"Be careful," Parker tells me before skillfully getting on his camel as if he does this every day. I stare at him with my mouth open. "I used to have a horse." He says sheepishly. I shake my head with a smile and get helped up onto the camel. I hold on as tightly as possible.

The man grabs my leg to steady me for a second.

"Hands off my girl!" Parker calls out, guiding the camel. People stare. I see someone with a large camera take a picture.

...paparazzi?

My attention shifts when Parker starts strangely doing the Harlem shake on his camel.

"You're going to fall, you idiot!" I yell at him.

"YOLO!" He shouts, and then falls, straight into a huge metal bucket-tub-like thing full of water.

"Why am I interested in this guy?"

"Let's talk," Parker demands, at the door.

"Parker! Get out!" I screech, pulling the towel tighter around me. He smiles and shuts the door behind him. I sigh. "What do you want?"

"What I want... is for you to go on a date with me."

Chapter 16

"W-what? Parker, I only have a towel on right now, why the hell would you ask me- no demand this- at a moment like this?" I ask him with wide eyes, back to the wall in shock.

"Yeah, I am pretty turned on right now."

"Parker!" I screech. His lips tug in a lazy, dimpled, sexy smile. He runs a hand through his hair, making it even messier.

"Ally, get dressed, and we'll talk." He says in an authoritative tone. A very hot authoritative tone.

I nod silently, unable to speak, submissive. He walks out and shuts the door. I let out a breath and slowly slump to the ground.

Jesus, Ally, you need to snap out of this!

I get up and walk to my bag. I open it and quickly change into my soft cotton shorts and favorite tank top. I blow dry my hair and put it in a high ponytail before nervously walking out and into the living room of the hotel room where Parker stands with his back to me, facing the window, looking out.

I stare at him for a moment, and when his ears perk slightly, I can tell he's smiling.

"You, me, on a date, now," Parker says before turning around.

"Parker it's 10 at night and look what we're dressed in. That's so... Unplanned."

"Ally, everything that you do is always planned planned planned. I'm trying to teach you how to live, and people that live don't plan out every move that they make." He states with a smile.

"Yes, Parker, but I'm not them."

"Planned is overrated. Dates are usually planned out. If you're the opposite of them, you wouldn't plan on it happening, you'd just do it randomly because, in the real world, dates are planned for a specific time and place. So come on." He says.

Goddammit, does he always have to be right?!

"Parker I-"

"Before you try pulling the: 'I don't want this to ruin the friendship' card, I'm sorry, but shut the fuck up." He says, stepping towards me. "Ally, there's this thing between us, and I'm too blunt to not do anything about it. I believe wholeheartedly that we are meant to go on this date."

I stare at him before walking to him slowly. I take his face in my hands before leaning up and kissing him. He responds instantly, wrapping his arms around my waist and pulling me closer to his defined chest. Our lips move in sync with each other's, sending my heart into a frenzy, an electric buzz all over my skin.

Screw getting drunk! This is better!

I pull away a little, resting my forehead on his, on my tip toes. His eyes stay shut for a moment as he smiles.

"Girl. Y'all are fuckin' beautiful."

We turn to see Hendrik recording us from the side. I shake my head and he starts typing away. Soon enough both mine and Parker's phones are going off with the notification that Hendrik tagged us in a video of us kissing.

Parker looks at me as if waiting for an answer.

"Give me a moment to think," I tell him and awkwardly walk back to the bathroom, shutting the door behind me. I look in the mirror and start to low-key hyperventilate. I quickly put on foundation, eyeliner, and mascara within about three minutes of a Trap City song. I change into ripped jeans, a crop top, and a Nike windbreaker jacket - leaving it unzipped - and slip on a pair of white-on-black Adidas.

Ok. Basic white Tumblr trash outfit goals!

I nod before grabbing the phone and walking out.

"Gee. I assumed you were just contemplating how to get out the window without breaking anything." Parker states upon seeing me, now in khaki joggers, a university sweater, and Jordans. He takes my hand and pulls me out. He even opened the door to the car and the hotel for me.

He drives, to where? I don't know. I grab my phone and hook it up to the aux cord.

I put on Fabulous from High School Musical 2, to resurface the memory of our 'first kiss'.

He smiles and rests a hand on my thigh. It sends me inwardly freaking out. I don't know what a relationship even is! What do I do? I didn't plan for this to happen all of a sudden! What do I do?!

"Stop freaking out." He says, lightly squeezing my thigh for a second. "Just let this happen. Let us happen."

I relax in my seat put one of my hands over his, and play with his pointer finger. I look out the window into nothing. Next, I put on Wet Cigarette by Mars Argo.

Let's just see where the night takes us.

"YOUR AN IDIOT PARKER WEST!"

"JUST DO IT! YOU'RE IN A NIKE WINDBREAKER AND THEIR MOTTO IS JUST DO IT! NOW KILL IT!" He screams back from where he stands on the counter of the restaurant. People are recording, but I really couldn't give a fuck.

"UM excuse me! You're the man here!"

"Yes, but this place has a large kitchen, and women belong in kitchens and working and stuff so kill the damn spider!"

Well, we were eating, this was the best day of my life, but then suddenly a spider dropped onto our table. See, me and Parker both have a huge fright of spiders. So naturally, he jumped onto the counter, knocking over a napkin thing, and I onto the backrest of the booth we were in. Now, with people telling us to shut up or calm down, or petty threats, we were arguing on who kills it.

People are so dramatic, is it really an issue that we're yelling?! It's freaking 11 at night! Go to bed old hags!

"That was so sexist I have half the mind to slit your throat!"

"And what you said about me being the man here isn't?!"

I freeze.

"Okay, I see your point, but as the person who demanded I go on this date in the first place, kill it, or I don't go on any more dates, and you don't get kisses."

He flies towards the table and quickly kills the spider. He grabs a napkin, saying "ew ew ew ew ew ew" on the way to the trash with the dead spider n-

a scream resonates from Parker, where baby spiders start to crawl over his arm, going all over him. I scream as well.

"NOT THE SEXY BODY I ADORE!" I scream, grabbing the booze hose and spraying the spiders off of him.

At least to say, the restaurant is now trashed.

"THAT'S IT! OUT OF MY RESTAURANT NOW!"

Me and Parker make a run for it, and we scramble into his car. There were no cameras inside or out, so we should be in the clear. The manager with a cell phone in hand screams at us as we take off.

When we get back to the apartment, Parker instantly goes for the bathroom, ignoring Hendrik and his boyfriend who stare at us with confusion.

"Just.. Don't ask."

I take off my shoes and jacket and climb into bed. I snuggle into Parker's scent. The lights flicker off and I see Hendrik and + get in their respectful bed. Parker eventually comes out of the bathroom freshly showered, smelling of Axe, only in a pair of basketball shorts.

H O T.

He climbs in and stares at me. I open my eyes fully finally and look back. He smiles.

"Can I hold you?" He asks as if he's a child asking for candy. I nod slowly. He pulls me to him, wrapping his arms around my waist. He puts his head on my neck.

Does he hear my pulse?

"Can I kiss you?" He whispers. I nod again. He presses a light kiss to my neck, then my jaw, then my lips. He smiles against my lips and lies down again with me against him. Then, a quick, three taps against the door, followed by:

"Parker West and Allison Smith! We know you're in there! It's the police, open up!"

"Shit."

"Oooh long days, spent wasting awaaaay! Get me out of here, Mommy, Daddy, please please, aussi, wi wi, I need to pee-pee!" Parker sings.

"Shut the fuck up." I groan loudly. We are currently in a waiting cell. Luckily, my brother was only a few towns over and would be here in about five minutes. Parker marks minutes down on the wall with chalk he found.

"I wanna go hhhoooommme oohh ohh hhooommee, I wanna go hooome!" He sings straight out of Spongebob.

"Why am I dating you?" I ask myself more than him. He looks over and smiles.

"So we're dating now?" He asks, approaching quickly and leaning over me. My eyes widen as I take in what I just stated.

"I mean- uh - I just.. I-"

He cuts me off with a kiss. "I'm kidding Ally. Jeez. I was going to ask you momentarily. Way to steal my roll there." He sighs.

He lies next to me and pulls me to him. I sigh.

"Allison Smith you are dead!"

"Shit!"

"Who are you again?" Ty asks Parker.

"Parker.. My boyfriend." I state meekly. His eyes widen.

"You're only 19 Ally!"

"There's a girl who just got knocked up at 19 Ty, this is my first relationship, and it legit just started like an hour ago so let's not start?" I say angrily. "Listen," I say breathing out, "I'm sorry you had to drive all the way out here. But please, give me a break. It was all a spider's fault."

He pinches the bridge of his nose.

"Fine. Just this once because this is the first thing bad you've done. Hell, you've never even drunk before. I should be glad."

Parker and I share a look.

"Oh, there's the look. See you ratted yourself out. You have drank. Jesus Ally, what the hell?"

"Wow for someone who hates when I swear you sure use your words pretty loosely."

"That's different, I'm like, your dad as much as that makes me cringe." He states. I roll my eyes at him.

"You're going to be a dad in a few months anyway. What's the big deal? You're my brother. B r o t h e r. Take a chill pill. If I start going haywire and become a badass smoking, drinking, tattoo-full person then blame it on our biological dad."

"You've smoked and you have a tattoo? That's funny."

I sigh.

"I have a duckling tramp stamp," I admit. He lets out a harsh breath.

"We are going to talk, Ally. I don't need this AGAIN."

"Again?" Parker asks, confused.

"Oh, you haven't told your lil' boyfriend, Al?"

"Ty, do not be a douchebag right now," I demand, stressing, not wanting Parker to find out my ages-old secret.

"Ally, I think he has a right to know," Ty says with a slightly cocky expression.

"He does, he does, I don't want to tell him now. Please, Ty."

"This is your punishment, Ally."

"Ty."

"When she was the wee age of.. oh.. 14? 15? Ally was addicted to heroin."

I move away from a totally-fucking-shocked Parker, as far as possible. I rest my head on the window as I already feel the tears building. "She'd gotten it from a total douchebag guy. He was a hockey player. He convinced her into it. See, Ally is gullible and easily convinced. Her fatal flaw. Addicted. Not for too long. About three months before I found out and packed up and moved. Even had to go into rehab for three weeks. It was bad. I could tell something was different."

Parker looks frozen. Slowly, he turns his head towards me. "Ally?"

I let my hair fall in the way to act as a curtain. "Ally."

My body twitches for a second, and I know what's coming. I shout at Ty to pull over. He does. I get out and grab onto the guardrail, heaving slightly, waiting for the puke to finally come to me. It doesn't, which shocks me, and I slowly sit on the ground. I put my head against the rail and breathed deeply, my hair blocking my face from sight, letting it stay a secret that I was crying.

"Ally," Parker's voice reaches me. I glance through my hair to see him crouch beside me. He moves my hair out of my face and turn my head towards him. He smiles lightly. "I don't care about something that was like 5 years ago. It's okay." He whispers. I blink rapidly. He leans down and kisses me softly. I nod when he pulls away. He helps me into the car. Ty looks a bit guilty. I curl up, feeling tired as hell.

"Go to sleep, Flower. I'll make sure everything will be okay."

"Okay."

Chapter 17

"I missed you so much you cutie little baby," Parker says to Jordan as he takes him in his arms.

"Wow, but you didn't say this to me when we spent two days apart two weeks ago," I say sarcastically. He shoots me a look. I smile, lean up, and kiss him. He sets Jordan down in his crib and pulls me to him.

"I missed you so much you beautiful woman." He says while looking me in the eyes. I smile in satisfaction and rest my head on his chest.

"Finally, my O.T.P." A sighing voice of Laney says happily.

"I thought your otp was Kehlani and Ryder," I state with confusion. She puts a finger to her lips.

"Shh. Just let it happen." She says. Parker lightly kisses my neck and breathes in my scent.

I never understood couples. Why they were always kissing, hugging, touching, and holding hands 24/7? Now that I'm with Parker, it's understandable. It's this pull, this gravitational force that just makes you want... need... crave to be touching them in the littlest of ways, any ways possible. It's hard to be apart because they're the only thing to consume your mind and you just want to be next to them, feeling their skin, knowing that they are safe beside you.

Or maybe that's just me and my abandonment issues..?

"Babe I have an idea," I tell him, leaning back.

"What's that?" He asks with a light and curious tone.

"Let's find an organization online for saving ducks and make a donation."

His eyes light up and he nods. He picks Jordan up as I make my way to my laptop. We find one in a matter of minutes, but suddenly Parker is gasping. I look over to see him holding one of Jordan's arms. "What's wrong?" I ask quickly.

"Look! Ally what's happening to him?!" He asks upon showing me the tiniest feather on earth. It's a tiny little white one. I smile.

"He's going through puberty, babe," I explain in the easiest way possible. A bright smile graces his features, a wide one, making me happy just looking at it, and he laughs, which makes me captivated instantly. Like bells, making my heart warm and melt.

It scares me, what I feel for him. But at the moment, my focus was on his laugh. All I could do was stare, my head slightly tilted. Eventually, he notices. "You're staring." He whispers. I take note that Jordan had flown out of his hands as I let my eyes rake over Parker. "Still staring." He says. I push him against the dresser and kiss him suddenly. He smiles, and flips us around, picking me up and setting me on top of the dresser before standing between my legs and kissing me roughly.

Our lips move better in sync than the band.

Slowly, perfectly, our kiss is passionate, filled with want, greed, and need. I rake my nails down his back, and he groans. I bury my head in his neck and he starts kissing the exposed skin on my neck.

Perfect timing for his friends to walk in yelling:

"EEEYooo."

Parker jumps away from me in shock. I fix my shirt and hair awkwardly. "Oh." They all say again.

"Explain," Leroy demands.

"Have you guys been smashing this whole time?" Danny asks, his voice raised a pitch. I choke on the air for a second. It takes skill to do that, you know.

"No, you idiots." Parker snaps. "We officially started dating while we were away."

They all say "oooooh" together. Parker helps me down.

"We got arrested for destruction of private property. It was fun." Parker says. I shake my head and go back to the computer. I put in my credit card info and donated ten dollars. Apparently, I'm going to be shipped a water bottle with a picture of a duckling and a T-shirt. "Ooh! Ooh! I call the water bottle!" Parker yells in excitement.

"What?! No! I paid the cash, I get the.. damn it I'm so bad with rhymes... stuff.. yeah. Stuff." I say pathetically. He gives me a blank look. I narrow my eyes. "Fine. It's only because you're bringing me to McDonald's as our second date. Maybe we won't get it trashed." I mutter. I grab Jordan's little harness and leash and start to strap him up. Parker helps, and I hate but love the way that when our hands brush together, I get a buzzing feel on my skin.

We all start walking outside, and a smile graces my features.

My happiness is soon turned to anger.

"That.... vulture," I say angrily as some basic, trashy-looking girl hits on Parker. She even hugs him. He's so oblivious! He waves over to the table while grabbing the drinks. He invited her over here?!

I stand, grab the first person there, and smash my lips against hers.

I pull back. "You're a great kisser." That is all I tell her. She blinks before kissing me again and slipping me her number before walking off, waving shyly as she leaves the shop.

"Plot twist Ally is lesbian," Jose says, breaking the ice as I inspect the number.

"What. The. Hell." Parker growls out. I look over.

"Hmm?" I ask innocently. His jaw is clenched, portraying his anger.

"Polly, this is Ally, my girlfriend. Ally, this is my little sister, Polly."

Ooooh..... oops.

"Hi," I say to her. "Calm down babe," I drawl, "it's a part of the list. I'm straight, I mean example, this morning-"

"My sister is right here Ally!" He snaps at me.

"Geez. All we did was kiss and she's like 17, I think she understands." I say, laughing. I smile at him. He sighs before opening his arms. I duck into his warmth and hum in contentment. His sister gushes.

"I'm confused but you guys are cute." His sister says.

"I know, I know. We are adorable just as we are." He says, caressing my cheek.

God, he'll be the death of me.

Chapter 18

"Babe.", Parker whispers as my jaw clenches. He's so annoying. "Psst! Babe! Babe! It's important."

"WHAT?!" I finally scream at him. Everyone in the class taking the test falls silent and turns to look at us as I glare at Parker.

He smiles.

"Do you have any gum?" He asks cheekily. Other people start to glare at him for disrupting the class. "Well, I can't kiss you with decaf coffee breath." He states. Everyone starts looking at each other, whispering.

"Yooo you guys finally together?!" One of his fake friends yells over. Parker tries to wrap an arm around my shoulder but I push him off.

"Why her?"

"She's so... nerdy."

"Whatshisface, Brady? Braden? I don't know. He said she had modeling pictures that someone had shown him. I guess she's wicked hot under those.. layers."

"I mean at least she doesn't dress like a slut."

I stand by that last comment.

"Who said that? That I do- Parker if you poke my ass one more time" I growl. He stops. "That I don't dress like a slut?"

Everyone points to a girl with pastel pink hair and a baby blue dress on. "Sup?" She asks.

"Let's be friends. Meet me at the Starbucks on Third Street after class." I demand boldly. She shrugs and nods.

I love how our teacher stays passed out, and disinterested. This is just a pop quiz. He said himself he doesn't put it in our grades, so oh well. Parker suddenly pulls me onto his lap and kisses me intensely. I kiss back instantly, finding joy in this kissing thing.

"GET IT WEST!" A bunch of his friends yell out. The teacher wakes up. He looks at us. He blinks before going back to bed.

I shrug and kiss Parker again. He tickles my side and I giggle in delight.

"Let's skip class." He says. I nod and get off his lap. We get our things. Everyone watches as we walk out. Parker smacks my ass just before we walk out.

"I'm getting this out there." I hear some girl say. I pretend not to see Parker give her a thumbs up.

So we were holding hands, walking, when fate decided to hit.

"Ally?"

I freeze. Parker looks at me, confused. He looks to the guy off to my side, then back to me.

"Ally Smith." I turn to the guy. "It's great to see you after all these years."

Anger bubbles in my chest. This is the first time I've seen him since.. Her.

"I couldn't say the same about you," I say in a low tone, my hand squeezing Parker's.

"Ally, who's this?" Parker asks, concerned. I let out a breath.

"Remember how I told you that I found the body of my best friend who'd committed suicide due to her boyfriend cheating?" I ask him. He nods. "This was her boyfriend." His eyebrows raise, and his eyes widen.

"Wow, so I get to meet the douchebag who put my baby through pain. Nice." Parker says sarcastically, glaring at Connor.

"You're in a relationship? Wow. Congrats Al. Really. I didn't think you'd want a relationship." He says. "And you look great by the way. You glowed up."

I cringe as I remember looking at myself in the mirror every night and sometimes even crying because I hated how I looked. With acne, braces, glasses, and no good fashion sense whatsoever, I was often a target for bullying.

"Whatever," I mutter. I start to walk away with Parker.

"Wait! Ally! I was actually looking for you."

I freeze again, angry.

"Well, what the fuck do you want then?!"

"Wow, you finally said fuck." He mutters to himself as he gets a few papers out of his bag. "Uh, something with Melinda came in from the government. I was asked to deliver these two things to you. One is something of Mel, the other is from.. your dad."

Stiffly, I take the two papers from him.

"I hope I'll see you around.. and.. I'm sorry. For everything that I did."

It wouldn't be until later that I'd find out he committed suicide, going on this wooden bridge for trains. He'd let it hit him.

"I should open it. I shouldn't. I should. I shouldn't."

"Just open it, Ally," Parker tells me.

"Ok," I say and pick up my father's first.

I blow out a slow breath as I open it. Parker looks at me curiously.

Allison,

Hey. It's been a while since I last wrote you. I wrote you on your graduation day. I don't know if you read it or not. Before that, it was the night of your prom. Every birthday since your tenth.

I wish I knew you. I wish I hadn't been so stupid. It wasn't your fault what happened to your mother. I know that now. Its nature. I shouldn't have abandoned you and your brother. I'm so sorry. I'm so proud of both of you.

I've seen some of the modeling jobs you and your brother have done together. You grew up to be such a beautiful young woman. I saw a college basketball game the other day, and I saw you. You're the assistant coach. I heard of the things you have done for the team. I'm so damn proud.

I know you may not be happy to hear this or may be upset, but I'm coming to the game tonight.

I hope to meet you. I want to know you, Ally.

See you.

Love you, Dad.

I lift my gaze and stare at the wall.

Maybe if this had been a couple of years ago, I'd have been angry, and tearing it up. But I lost Melinda. I have Parker, who makes me see clearer.

I'm going to forgive him. Life is too short to hold grudges this long. While I can never really forgive Connor, I can forgive my father because some people don't get to meet their dads ever, and there's a little girl inside me somewhere wanting a father.

A tear drops from my eye and lands on the paper. Parker takes in a sharp breath. He takes the paper from me and reads it. I pick up Melinda's.

But I can't open it.

I set it back down to read after the game.

I stand and go to walk towards my room, but Parker pulls me into his arms. I hug him back, a smile gracing my features.

I pull away and shake my head, smiling at him, and say, "You're an idiot."

He smacks my ass, saying, "Come on, we gotta go."

"You are very touchy-feely today. You keep smacking my ass. It's annoying. Kind of." I tell him.

"You like it, don't you?" He asks with a smile as he takes my hand and we walk into the gym again. Crowds are starting to walk in. After practice we'd had about half an hour to do what we wanted so we got Starbucks.

I blush and look away. "Don't be embarrassed. It's my fault. Well, not really... I mean... It's not my fault you have one beautifully, perfectly thick ass." He says in my ear. I feel my blush deepen. I shake my head and walk away from him. He laughs and joins his friends. Me and the coach go over tactics for the game plan before deciding which to use that would be better against this certain team.

Created by Moi.

I smile at the coach before walking over to the water bottles for the team and where I'd placed Parker's gummies. I bend over to grab them, and of course, a smack goes on my ass. I freeze before standing up. I turn around slowly. From the corner of my eye, I see my dad watching with his eyes widened.

Parker smirks at me. I slap him across the face. I look over to where my dad is. He fidgets nervously. I wave with a smile. My face is turned towards a pissed-looking Parker.

"That was rude." He says, looking wicked angry. So I ran. I duck under flying basketballs and the occasional arm as he chases me, but he eventually catches up and turns me towards him.

I mean, we probably look like a couple that has abuse going on right now because I see a few older men standing up and walking toward us.

That is until Parker kisses me. I wrap my arms around his neck and smile. He suddenly picks me up, and I squeal in delight.

"Coming through, make way for my queen here, boys." He says, and his friends chuckle while moving out of the way. I smile happily as he carries me back to the supplies. He sets me down and kisses my nose. I blush. "You're so cute when you blush." He says, making me blush harder. "Now where's my gummies?"

I blink.

"You are a douchebag," I say, laughing, and grab the gummies off the floor. I hand them to him. He jumps in excitement and opens them. He pulls out the red dinosaur one first and starts talking.

"Oh, you're all bloody. Did someone do that to you? Did someone eat your head off like this?!" He asks the dinosaur before biting off the head and laughing darkly to himself.

"Wow, I am dating a psychopath," I state, recording him. He looks up. He pours the gummies all in his mouth at once, drops the trash left onto the table, and grabs my phone. He swallows the gummies as I hop down.

"No! Ally give me the phone!" He shouts at me. He gets my arm.

"TRE!" I yell. He turns towards me. I throw him the phone. He catches it. Parker runs for him and I get on the sidelines. Tre eventually tosses it to Derrick, who tosses it to Nate, who tosses it to Jose, who tosses it back to me. I laugh easily as I run while posting it on Instagram. Then Snapchat. Then Facebook.

"ALLY!" Parker yells. "I'M GOING TO KILL YOU!"

"YOU CAN'T DO THAT, I'M YOUR GIRLFRIEND!" I shout back. I stop running and stand still, only for him to collide with my back, knocking both of us to the floor. He catches himself with his hands while I lay facing him. He just stares at me. I stare back.

"..kiss her, kiss her," oh my god no, "KISS HER KISS HER KISS HER KISS HER!"

He smiles and kisses me softly. Then, he grabs the phone, which I roll out of his grasp slickly and springs up.

"These people are fucking ninjas." I hear some chick say. "But... goals."

"Haha! I already posted it on Instagram, Snapchat, and Facebook, and now all that is left is Twitter, Tumblr, and YouTube!" I tell him.

"Ally, let's talk this out.."

"WHEN DO WE EVER TALK THINGS OUT?!" I yell at him. He stops and thinks for a second.

"Good point."

With that, he chases me again, but this time I have a plan. I run towards the bleachers where my dad sits and run up them. I sit next to him and wait for Parker to catch up.

"Babe, give me the phone. This is my social life you're ruining." He tells me. I smile.

"Parker, my father, my father, Parker."

Parker freezes before going into the 'perfect man on earth' act.

"Mr. Smith. It's so great to meet y- wait you're the one who a-"

"Dad, I forgive you and I'd love to have you in my life, and I'll see you after the game!" I say in a high-pitched tone before ducking under Parker's arm and running.

"UUUUGH" Parker groans.

From this day on, I vow to be more forgiving.

Chapter 19

So, my dad, Parker, and I were currently at a diner, it being pretty late now. We'd talked about anything, avoiding the subject that really needed to be spoken of, until my dad finally cracked.

"Ally, thank you for seeing me today. I'm surprised, actually. I-I thought you hated me and that you were going to slap me." He admits with a sheepish smile. I laugh.

"No. I was angry all my life, sure, but something happened a few years ago that made me realize I should be more forgiving. I should have contacted you much sooner. But really, I forgive you." I say with a smile, a huge weight lifted off my shoulders. He smiles and takes one of my hands.

"I... I need to be honest with you. I have a wife." He tells me. A jab goes through my heart, but I don't let it show. "And two kids." He says, pulling out his wallet. He shows me a picture of a woman standing beside him, a baby girl in her arms, and a baby boy in his. "About a year apart."

"You have a beautiful family," I tell him with a smile. I check the time and groan. "I have a test tomorrow. I need to go home and get some sleep. I'll call you.. is that okay?" I ask him. He nods quickly, standing, and hugging me.

"That's great, Al... I hope to see you soon?" He says in a questioning tone. I nod.

"Soon." I agree, and take Parker's hand, and we walk out. We get in his car. "Can I stay at your place tonight?" I ask, sighing. He nods and starts the car.

So what I have two outfits and a toothbrush at his place. It isn't a big deal.

"Are you okay?" Parker asks as we drive silently through the roads of the city.

"I'm fine," I assure him, squeezing the hand he has resting on my thigh. He doesn't respond, but telling by the expression on his face, he doesn't believe it. He pulls into his apartment complex, and we quietly get inside, or so I'd thought. Not quietly enough.

"Parker. West. It is practically the middle of the n- oh hey Ally- night."

"Sis, it's been a long day. Please." Parker begs. She sighs before going into her room. Parker starts to walk towards his room before he realizes I'm not following. He turns around slowly. I stare blankly at the wall.

Why weren't we good enough?

Was it only because of Mom?

Did he just not want us?

"Ally," Parker whispers and approaches slowly. The first tear spills. He pulls me to him. I wind my arms around his stony waist, appreciating his abs, but wishing he was actually squeezable for just a second.

I do a small laugh and sniff.

"Why does it even matter to me?" I ask, my voice sounding so vulnerable and broken, that I flinch at the sound of it. He leans back and caresses my cheek with the pad of his thumb, wiping away stray tears.

"Because it isn't fair." He murmurs. "You still manage to look so beautiful when you're crying."

So I do what any frustrated teenage hormonal girl would do when depressed.

I kiss him.

He kisses back, and it's a soft, but slow and drugging kind of kiss. The type you get high off of, see the moon and stars, the sun and earth all mold into one being.

I pull away, resting my head on his. I smile, and he opens his eyes and meets mine.

"Come on, let's get some sleep."

I woke earlier than Parker and got an idea. I smile and slowly get out of his bed to not wake him up. After changing, brushing my teeth, and getting a little bit of makeup on so I don't look dead, I go into the kitchen.

I look around, finding pancake batter, eggs, and bacon. I smile and start getting to work.

After about twenty minutes, I hear a sniffing sound while I'm flipping a pancake. I smile.

"Ooooh" Parker says, going to grab a piece of bacon. I slap his hand and turn the stove off. I set three plates, putting one in the microwave for whatever time his sister wakes up.

He wraps his arms around my waist from behind. "You are incredible." He murmurs in my ear. I smile and turn with his plate, giving it to him. He smiles and takes it, muttering a thanks before stuffing bacon in his mouth and moaning loudly.

I smile and eat with him, sitting across from him with my laptop in front of me, along with my credit card, on the website.

I buy the tickets, pay for the night's stay, put in information, and smile largely when I'm done buying me and Parker tickets to Disney.

"Whatcha doin' there?" Parker asks as he takes my empty plate. I turn the computer around.

"You free on December 23rd?" I ask him.

"That's... your... You're bringing me to Disney in Paris for my birthday?" He asks. I smile at him and nod. He jumps up from his seat and comes over to me, pulling me in his arms and lifting me from the ground. I squeal in excitement. He laughs, hugging me tightly.

"Wait that means we only have four days to pack." He states.

"Three. We do have a plane to catch the day before."

"Then let's get going!"

A week's worth of outfits for two nights' stay, check.

Adidas sneakers, Nike Pros shoes, heels, check.

Expensive dress for our date, check. Hopefully, it won't be a disaster this time.

Jordan at his babysitter's, check.

Mila and Kila in the care of Laney, check. The little poppy plant had another one grow, so we decided to name it Sheila, the daughter of Mila and Kila, a lesbian flower couple. #Pride.

Plane tickets, Disney tickets, mine and Parker's IDs because I don't trust him, and phone, check.

I get outside to see Parker sitting on the hood his car wearing Mickey Mouse ears, holding an extra set, but the other set has a bow on it. He hands it to me with a smile. I lean up and kiss him before tugging him down. I put them on to make him happy.

The whole way to the airport, he decides to listen to Britney Spears or Trap City to get him hyped, but about halfway there, I change it to a slow Taylor Swift song to get him calmed down. Sure enough, he passes out.

As I stop at a red light, I stare at his sleeping form, his perfect face with its peaceful expression, his lips twitching like he was having a good dream.

Staring at him, at that moment, was when I realized it.

That I'm falling in love with him. Very quickly and very hard.

I look back at the road and continue driving, but not before taking his hand in mine.

"This. Is. Lit. As. Fuck." Parker says, a huge smile on his face.

"Indeed." I agree, as he runs around the hotel. I move our bags towards the corner of the room.

"Be honest... Why did you do this for me?" Parker asks hesitantly, like he's nervous, scratching the back of his neck.

"Are you stupid?" I ask him. He nods. I laugh, shaking my head. "Parker, half of my list basically is complete because of you. Do you realize how grateful I am for that?" I ask him softly.

"I didn't really think about it." He admits. I smile and walk up to him. I take his face in my hands and kiss him softly.

"Now, let's go to the amusement park!"

Chapter 20

"I'm tireeeeed babe.", Parker whines as I throw him a towel.

We'd decided to call it quits on the roller coasters and go swimming while the fireworks happened. I'd rented out a public pool just for me and Parker.

I mean, it still counts.

And technically, I'd already been in a public pool: the one I'd had built for the basketball team and the rest of campus.

I approach him and wrap my arms around his neck. "So you don't want to see me in a bikini?" I ask, tilting my head slightly. His eyes widen.

"Let's go already, woman!"

"You're such a pervert," I mutter, going over to my bag and pulling out the bikini I got.

It's aqua colored. He inspects it, then nods. I roll my eyes and take the bikini back, going into the bathroom and changing. When I walk out, he puts a hand over his chest and shuts his eyes.

"Give me a second, you just keep taking my breath away." He states. I smile at his cheesiness, finding it charming and adorable, and ducking into his arms. He smiles against my neck, embracing me back.

"Shut up, you idiot." I giggle. I pull my arms around his neck again and just stare into his eyes. He smiles again. Finally, I softly press my lips to his.

He responds instantly, and it turns into one of those kisses where I know he's stable for me.

I can feel his emotion, the passion between us, and it's in these types of moments where I wonder if he's it for me, if he's the one person that'll never bring me pain, never hurt me, and love me unconditionally like I've always wanted.

Half of me says yes, and the other half screams no.

My heart says yes, that he's going to care about me and love me, but then there's that dark place in my mind that tells me I don't know, that he will wind up hurting me, that he'll meet someone prettier, smarter or dumber, someone who will give him their body easily because it isn't a big deal to them...

Or maybe I'm just being irrational.

He pulls away, a confused look on his face.

"What's wrong?" He asks. I shake my head, dismissing these thoughts.

"Nothing." I try to assure him, but it obviously doesn't work.

"Ally, our relationship is built of off me seeing 50 secrets of yours. I know your secrets, you know most of mine, the others I'm not just ready to tell you yet, so please, be honest with me?" He asks. I nod.

"You make me feel this way that I've never felt before, and.. I'm scared... not of the feeling, but that you're going to find someone prettier or smarter or even dumber and you'll leave me like everyone else." I whisper. He shakes his head, laughing.

"Ally, I want to assure you that that is never going to happen. One, you're literally a model, so obviously there isn't going to be ANYONE prettier than you. To me, you're even more gorgeous than other people will ever see you as. You have top grades, better than anyone's in our school except Aiden Rule, which, we all know he's a fucking.. never mind. That isn't important. Anyway, in a way, you're pretty stupid too."

"Hey!"

"Hear me out. You're stupid in a way that I like. It's more of oblivious, and innocent. You don't know how to do a lot of things because you've never done them before. And I love that. I love how innocent you are. It makes me feel needed, and men like to feel needed." He states.

"Why?"

"We just kind of do. Not only that, I love your little nose, and your aqua-colored eyes fuck me up every time our eyes meet, I love your perfect lips, your perfect smile, your long black hair, and your knock-out body. I love every single little thing about you. So don't you ever worry about me finding someone else because that's impossible."

He wipes a stray tear out of the corner of my eyes and pulls me into his arms.

"Come on, let's go to the pool before the fireworks start."

"Okay."

We got a worker to take a few pictures of us in the pool, like a photo shoot. My favorite was of him standing, my legs wrapped around his waist, his head on my shoulder, facing out towards the camera, his eyes closed, me having one arm dropped, the other wrapped around his neck, my hand in his hair.

In the background, the Disney castle stood tall, fireworks perfectly bursting.

I posted it everywhere when we got back to our hotel. He posted a different one of a similar position, but we were kissing in that one.

We were now sitting on our balcony, me wrapped in a fuzzy robe, him in sweats, showcasing his perfectly muscular chest and abdomen.

"You're really hot," I state, taking a sip of my tea after. He smirks, a happy glint on his face.

"I can say the same about you." He replies.

"You can't even see me right now."

He reaches out to the drawstring of my robe, grabs it, but stops, and looks up at me for permission. I smile and raise an eyebrow, challenging him. He pulls it to reveal the black and aqua-colored lingerie set I'd gotten for this moment.

His eyes widen, and I note how his breathing increases.

"Uh.. woah." He murmurs to himself as I stand. I shake off the robe and sit on his lap. "Ally." He whispers, and I feel something on my thigh.

"Can you get you're wallet out of your pocket? It'll ruin the moment."

"That isn't my wallet." He squeaks.

"Oh."

I laughed once. "Parker, I'm going to be blunt here... I'm falling in love with you. Quick, and hard. That didn't sound right... Anyway, I know what I want. I want you. I trust you." I tell him.

"Are you sure?" He asks, his eyes still widened.

"Yes. I trust you, and that you're not going to hurt me too much." I whisper. He nods.

"Ally, just to get this clear, you're not the only one falling."

And with that, he kisses me, and from that kiss, becomes so much more.

"Happy birthday, Parker."

I wake the next morning, a smile on my face, the smell of food filling my senses.

A sore feeling is between my legs, and I blush as I remember the previous night.

I pull the blanket around me and inspect the room. Some things were knocked on the floor, and feathers litter randomly around. My hair was slightly damp.

Somehow we managed to go from the bed to the shower, back to the bed. Beside me are a nicely folded bra, underwear, crop top, leggings, a pair of socks, and my Converse. I change while still sitting.

Laziness has perks.

When I finally stand, I practically collapse.

"Ow." I hiss. I hear footsteps approach.

"Are you okay?" Parker asks me, kneeling. I blush.

"I can barely walk," I tell him, my blush increasing.

"That's an ego and confidence booster." He mutters, smiling as he helps me stand and puts an arm around my waist to keep me up.

"Shut up," I reply. "I can't walk because of Parker Junior over here."

"Yeah maybe so, but Ally Junior wasn't exactly complaining last night." He states, a huge smile on his face. "I remember something along the lines of: 'harder baby.. yeah, right there. Fuck you're good at th-'"

I slap a hand over his mouth.

"Stop," I command. He nods, still smiling.

"This." He finishes his sentence, blurting it out as if he can't help it. I shake my head, sighing, grimacing in pain as he sets me down on a chair. "I'm sorry."

"For what?" I question as he sets a plate of food in front of me. "Thank you," I murmur, picking up my fork.

"For hurting you." He says, sitting and looking at his plate. I reach over and lift his chin. He meets my gaze. Guilt shows in his expression.

"I asked for you to go harder. Be proud, Parker." I tell him, blushing and smiling. He laughs once takes my hand from his face and intertwines our fingers.

"You were amazing last night." He tells me and kisses my hand softly.

"I can definitely say the same," I reply with a cheeky smile. His smile lifts even more.

"You're cute." He states randomly.

"Parker, shut up."

Chapter 21

Everyone needs a person.

Someone they feel won't give up on them, no matter the circumstances.

That's what Parker is for me. He's the definition of the only thing I trust.

When you break trust, you're left with nothing to show for yourself, and luckily, Parker hadn't broken my trust since the day I met him.

Yet.

But I guess we'll see where the future will take us.

For now, all I want to worry about is how I'm going to get from this damned bed to my bags so I can get dressed for our date.

I sit up slowly, and stare at my bag, all the way across the room.

Maybe, just maybe if I summon the devil, will he throw the bag my way? Probably not. I'm probably too innocent for the likes of a demon.

Well, not too much anymore.

Okay, you know what? I'll just stand up and get it. It shouldn't be that bad. Then again, after the pain of losing my virginity in the first place went away, Parker had become ruthless seeing as I was enjoying it. Worth the moments I tell you.

I grab onto the table beside me and heave myself up. I wince, but after a minute or two of standing there, I'm okay, it's isn't as bad as I'd thought.

I smile in satisfaction and slowly make my way over. I grab the bag and put it on the bed before pulling out the shimmery red dress, red heels, and matching suit and tie for Parker.

I quickly change, and make my way to the bathroom, finding it easier to walk with every step I take. All in good time, they say.

I do my makeup with sparkles to match the shimmery dress. I left Parker's suit on the bed, so when he walks in with messy hair and a suit, I can't help but want a repeat of last night.

He whistles. "Let me tell you, my girl is so beautiful." He says to someone on a video call with him. "I'm gonna marry her." He tells the person.

"What does she look like?" A male voice asks.

"Brother, she's a class-A beauty. See." He taps and I know the camera is on me.

The guy whistles lowly. "Parker, how the hell did you get a model to date you?"

"You know about my work?" I question.

"Yeah. Of course. I live in London." He states. I've done lots of photo shoots there.

"Oh, that's cool."

"Parker, be a dear and introduce your brother to your girlfriend." The guy says.

Parker comes over. "Ally, this is my older brother Barry. Barry, my girlfriend Ally."

"Nice to meet you," I tell him with a smile.

"You as well. So Parker, how'd you get a girl like that?" He asks. Parked shrugs.

"I don't know. Let's ask Ally."

"Well, Parker, you broke me out of my shell enough to trust someone again, crossed a bunch of things off my bucket list, and just make me happy," I tell him with a smile.

"That's so sweet," Barry says.

Parker smiles at me. "Well Barry I gotta go take my lovely woman on a date now, so I'll talk to you later, okay?"

"You got it, brother."

They exchange I love you and then hang up. Parker sets his phone down before kissing my red lips deeply, his hands coming to my waist and pulling me to him. It shocks me at first but I work with him in the kiss.

"You look a little too beautiful." He tells me. "You should probably change."

"What?" I ask.

"I don't want other men looking at what is mine. Change." He tells me seriously.

He's serious.

"No. I don't care if men look at what's yours. Millions of men and women in other countries look at what's yours. What's two others?" I question. His eyes go into a darker shade of hazel.

"Two others that are in front of me that I get to punch." He says. I laugh lightly. "I don't like these lingerie photo shoots. I'm a selfish man, Ally, and I want you all to myself and the very fact that some creepy ass man has jerked off to you somewhere.."

His hands go into fists.

I wrap my arms around his neck.

"But Parker, they aren't the ones allowed to be inside me. With me. Holding my hand. Hugging me. Kissing me. Only you, baby." I whisper. He tucks his head in my neck and breathes in deeply.

"I guess. But like, I wanna be the only one that sees this perfect body. I mean, look at you. You got this thick ass, your bra size is 38C, and you have abs... No normal woman has these qualities. And men get to see that. And I wanna be the only one to see that because you're mine. Mine." He says.

I smile at him.

Suddenly, he rests his hand... Down there.

"This is mine," he whispers. My eyes widen. His hand goes to my chest. "This is mine." His hand goes to my face and he rests his hand on my cheek. "You're all mine. And I'm so lucky."

"I could say the same, Parker." I smile, laughing lightly.

"Yeah?" He asks.

The cocky ass just wants me to say what I like about him.

So I do exactly what he did. My hands float down his body and between his legs.

"This is mine," I say, smirking. His eyes widen and he fidgets uncomfortably.

Very quickly, I feel his pants stretch.

Damn it. He ruined it!

I break into laughter, slapping the counter. "I didn't even get to finish!" I exclaim and laugh louder.

"I wouldn't if I were you." He says with a strained voice.

So I do continue. I rest my hand on his abs. "This is mine," I state. He takes a deep breath. I reach around and cup his ass all of a sudden. "This too." I state casually before putting my hand on his jawline."You're mine. Don't you forget it?" I murmur and press my lips to his. He kisses back softly.

"We gotta get to our date, Mrs.Perfection," Parker murmurs against my lips.

"So let's go, Mr.Perfection," I reply. We set our phones down and leave together, not wanting to be disrupted.

We walk together, hand in hand towards the restaurant, people around us getting out of our way because of the tour guide in front of us.

I see someone to the side taking a photo.

This place is amazing. I love it.

"Ooh. This place is so nice." Parker says. "This is the nicest place I've ever been to." He whispers as we step inside. I smile.

"Nicer will come, nicer will go." I wave it off. He looks around as we're led to our table. Fellow rich people look at us quickly before going back to their dinners, deciding we seemed to belong.

We sit across from each other. They get our orders for drinks instantly and come back after only a minute.

The tour guide leaves.

"God damn, I wish I could get a photo of you right now." Parker mumbles. I take the Polaroid camera out of my purse and hand it to him. He smiles and lifts the camera. I rest my chin on my hand and smile at him softly.

I take one of him as well and then put everything away.

What a perfect human being.

"This is our fifth date." He states.

"Yes," I reply, smiling.

"Personally, I think the McDonald's one was the second best. The first one was obviously the best but you get it." He says with a smile. I laugh quietly.

"Parker, what did you mean by you have secrets that you didn't want me to know?" I ask quietly.

He sighs. "I said that I wasn't ready to tell you but the truth is that I am ready, I just don't want you to see me differently." He states.

"I'd never."

"When I was really little, my... My dad killed my mom, Ally." He reveals. I take in a shocked breath. "He shot her, shot my older brother, and my older sister and he spared me but then he shot himself."

I take his hand, my heart feeling in physical pain for him.

"My mom died. My siblings obviously did survive, and my dad is dead. We were taken in by an adoptive single father, whose wife passed away from cancer. I don't remember what it was like to have a mother." He tells me.

"I know exactly how you feel," I say, kissing his hand softly.

"And that's what I love about you. You get me." He says. Stroking his thumb over my hand.

"Ooh the topic of what you love about me! Tell me more!" I say jokingly. He laughs and places my hand on his mouth, kissing the back of it softly.

"I love how much you trust me. I love your long black hair and how you get frustrated in the morning when you can't get your brush through the snarls. I love your perfect smile and your lips and how you smile when I kiss you. I love your aqua-colored eyes for obvious reasons and it's definitely one of the things that drew me to you when we first met in that Starbucks. I saw your eyes and I was a goner, baby. You were wearing all these layers and I didn't even see your amazing body until a little later on and it was already after I started catching feelings so that's how I know you're just it for me. It didn't take an amazing body for me to be drawn to you. That's just a plus. I'd love you even if you were 300 pounds. Because I love you. I love you, Ally."

At this point, I am crying, with a smile though.

"I love you too." My voice cracks a little. All nervousness in Parker's face disappears.

His eyes start to water slightly and he kisses my hand again.

"Are you guys ready to order?"

"Aw, you totally ruined it." I complain on accident, letting it slip out,

"W-what?"

I laugh lightly, "Sorry. We were having a moment. We would like to order."

So we order, and wait for our meal.

Then comes the topic of the upcoming game. This determines whether or not our team goes to the finals or the championships.

Parker has an upcoming interview with the local news sports segment and is forcing me to come with him.

Our plates are set in front of us, and we thank the waitress.

Over dinner, we talk about various things while Parker steals bits of my food because he finished mine. He makes small affectionate gestures which may not seem like a lot to him but it's a lot to me.

To go from having this completely empty feeling inside to having... I can't even explain it other than having everything I've ever needed and wanted... It's incredible.

People say that money can't buy happiness. Sure, money is fabulous. It can buy you amazing things. But it doesn't fill the void of having no loving attention.

My brother at the age of 17 did an amazing job of raising a child. I do not doubt in my mind that he'll be an amazing father to his twins on the way.

But due to having no mother figure, I didn't know what to do for most of my life until Melinda came into the picture. She showed me a lot. How to do my makeup, how to wax, and how to do my eyebrows nicely, practically showed me how to be a woman.

But it didn't fill the hole I had inside of me for my entire life.

Maybe this doesn't make sense.

Maybe I'm just being selfish, but I felt like I needed something.. Someone else to make me feel truly happy.

That's what Parker is for me. He's the epitome, the very paragon of all things happiness. Even when he's sad and down, he makes me happy because I just... I just love him.

"Are you okay?" Parker asks me as we walk back to the hotel.

"Yeah, why?"

"You spaced out there. Looked like you were thinking pretty hard." He explains.

"I was just thinking about you, and my past, and how you make me so, so happy," I tell him as he opens the door. He lets me in first and shuts the door behind him, and as he's locking it, I let my dress slip off of my shoulders, and down my hips.

He's struggling with the lock because it won't turn and that's okay because it gives me time to readjust the very scandalous lingerie I have on.

Parker sighs once it's locked and then turns towards me. He steps back in shock, his back against the door. His eyes are widened, and I try not to laugh as I take out my Bobby pins and let my hair fall around me.

And then I jump against him, winding my legs around his waist, my arms to his neck.

"Now, let me make you happy." I smile.

"I mean I was happy before but whatever you say."

I smile and kiss him.

And from there, it goes much further. Again. And again. And again.

Chapter 22

On the way home, we stopped and saw the Eiffel Tower, but didn't make a big deal of it.

We took a picture under it and we had to go because of the plane home.

We both missed Jordan too much to stay. We were there for a good three nights though, and it was the most special trip ever to me.

We rode first class, and the entire time, Parker slept. I just played with his hair for a while before turning on my phone when finally allowed and seeing my mass amounts of messages.

I check one from my brother first.

How was Disney with Lover Boy?

It was fun.

You guys didn't do anything, right?

Omg I'm an adult now give up on this

I'm gonna kick his ass

I then decide to leave that fun topic and go to Laney's messages to check up on Jordan.

Ally

Ally why aren't you answering

This is urgent!

It's about Jordan please answer

What happened?

I go into hyperventilation mode.

He found a friend. Not just any friend. I caught them smashing.

What?! Is he even old enough to have babies?!

You've had him for a few months now and he has all of his feathers in. I don't know how this works!

This isn't possible! I guess I'll have to break the news to Parker.

Oh no.

Oh yeah.

"Parker. Parker." I shake him awake. He opens his eyes and smiles at me.

"Hi, baby." He mumbles and kisses my nose.

"There's some... Not so good news."

His smile drops instantly. "What. Is it Jordan? My sister? Your brother? What is it, babe?"

"It's Jordan... I... Parker, you know that he's a teen now, and um... He... Laney caught him with a female. In a comprising position, if you understand what I mean." I whisper. Some lady in front of us turns around.

"Oh honey, your child went rogue and is whoring themselves out too? I know how you feel." The lady drawls in a drag queen voice and glares at her teen beside her who is texting and rolling her eyes.

"Ours is a pet duck... Not an actual kid. Jeez. That's kinda mean." I mutter.

"Tell me about it." The girl turns to me. "It's hypocritical. She lost her virginity at 14, mine at 18, to my steady boyfriend of 6 years and she's mad. Like whatever. Jesus."

I nod at her in appreciation.

"Good job," I tell her.

"Thank you. Someone gets it."

The lady glares before going back to what she was doing.

I now notice that Parker is frozen.

"Our.. Son... Lost his duckginity?"

"Yes, Parker. I'm sorry."

"I'm so proud of him." He whimpers and wipes a tear. "I told him, he could get the girl! I told him!"

"What?!" I spit out.

"Well, he and this one duck were lowkey getting frisky by the lake when I had him last weekend. And when we walked away I told him he was so hot enough to get her, I mean, who wouldn't want Jordan? He's the hottest duck around! He's got the feathers now, he's got that new sweater you made him that he looked totally fly in, and I got him some baby high tops from Dick's Sporting Goods that are Adidas and he was just looking great."

"What the hell is wrong with you?" I ask him.

"I don't know. You tell me. You're dating me."

"Yeah, and I still can't seem to figure it out here, okay?" I mutter.

"I'm offended."

"But I love you." I chirp in reply. He lets a smile break out and rests his head on my shoulder.

"I love you too, baby girl." He murmurs, making me melt inside.

"Y'all are too cute." The teen in front of us states, recording us. "Strive for this ladies and gents, a model and her basketball player boyfriend."

"You know us?"

"Hell ya. I go to the high school right now in the same city but you guys are big news all around." She says, tapping at her phone.

"Oh. I didn't know that." Parker says. "I mean I knew everyone looked at you because, well I mean look at my princess. Awe you're just so beautiful." Parker says, staring at me with a loving gaze. A blush creeps in my cheeks and I lower my gaze a little nervously. He laughs quietly.

"I'm so glad I got that on tape." That girl mutters. It's kind of creepy but me and Parker are both used to being on camera.

Parker chuckles. "I love you." He says quietly and rests his head on my shoulder again.

"And I love you, always, and forever."

From my mouth to the corner, to my cheek, to all along my jaw, Parker places kisses.

I was pinned to the wall, my legs around his waist. He had taken my wrists in his hands and pinned them to the wall as his lips went on a path downwards.

From quiet sighs to moans, I was enjoying myself wholeheartedly.

"Do you like that?" He laughs quietly in my ear, causing me to shiver.

I nod.

"Use your words, baby." He murmurs and bites my ear lobe lightly. I take in a breath.

"Yes."

"Goo-"

"AYEe-OH JESUS CHRIST!" Parker's friends all yell together and turn around.

"My virgin eyes... I'll never un-see it." His friend Jose says sickened.

"Start fucking knocking, idiots!" Parker grumbles angrily and gets my shirt on for me and puts on his. "Okay, you can turn around now."

They all do, holding their stomachs and pretending to be sick. Parker gives them each a handshake.

I mutter a hi, embarrassed. I pick up Jordan's new girlfriend who we named Addy because of Adidas, and I start getting her in her new pink collar.

See, we went and got them both their shots and we adopted Addy with papers. We can't have a depressed Jordan after all.

They kept snuggling. It was strange because they oddly reminded me of Parker and myself. Jordan was a strange case and always found doing weird things, and Addy was always following his lead into whatever.

I put Parker in his aqua blue collar and put them on their little leashes.

"You guys got another one?" Leroy asks.

"Yeah, Laney caught him and her smashing so we decided to adopt her," I tell them, and they laugh.

"Man got lucky when his father did too."

My gaze snaps to Parker instantly, who hisses at him to shut the fuck up, and then turns to me with a scared look.

"You told people? Really?"

"Um. Just these three. No one else, I swear. And maybe my sister."

"You told your fucking sister?! Parker, that's so awkward! Why would you do that?!" I ask him loudly.

"Because she guessed so! She said: "So did the birthday boy get luuuuucky? You did, didn't you? Oh, you're silent, you totally did!" He explains in a high-pitched girl voice. I take a seat on the bed and put my face in my hand. The ducks waddle over and run against my ankles in a sigh of comfort. I laugh as they squawk at me and I lean down and pet them.

"At least some people will comfort me and not lie," I tell them quietly, in a soft voice. Parker sighs.

"Great. Now because of you idiots, she's mad at me. Do you know what happens when she's mad at me? No physical contact whatsoever. No hand holding, no hugging, no arm around the waist or shoulder, no getting lucky now, no sitting too closely, no anything. And then she drags me to a photo shoot in which I have to watch where some creepy ass men are about to see my girl get basically naked for them."

"It's more for me than it is for them, Parker. Money is quite a luxurious thing. In my house, we were poor until my brother took up modeling. It's just a job, Babe." I tell him.

"I know. But I've explained this: I'm a selfish, very very selfish man. You're mine, okay?"

I sigh, "Okay."

Parker smiles and reaches to take my hand. I roll my eyes and hand him Jordan's leash before walking past him with Addy.

"Try again, babe."

Chapter 23

"You give me the type of feelings people write novels about," Parker says with a smile.

"Okay let up, what is this all about," I demand. "What do you want."

"Whatever do you mean?" He asks in a high-pitched voice.

"You've been being very verbally affectionate today and I know for a fact you prefer physically affectionate because you're not good with words, but you sure know how to use your hands." I remind him.

"Pfft..." He looks anywhere but me.

I raise my eyebrow.

"Fine. Come on, let's go inside."

"Parker I have tests to study for," I complain.

"And I have a surprise for you."

I grumble to myself, unlocking the door.

"Your dick is no surprise to me at this point, babe," I mutter at him.

I turn to the room to see everyone I care about inside with balloons, a cake, two bottles of wine, and shocked faces.

"Way to announce what we do when we're alone, Ally," Parker says, a devilish smile on his face.

"Well, you made it seem like.."

"Please. Stop." My brother says, cringing.

"Surprise?" Laney offers.

I grab the wine and get myself a glass quickly.

"Yeah! Surprise!" The jock part of the people here yells out. I start laughing and make greetings quickly, and someone turns on the music, and people start talking, everything going to course.

I look around the room. Banners and cheap streamers hang in the air. A cake is on the table.

Arms wrap around my waist.

"Sorry if it isn't too impressive. I've never thrown a birthday party before." Parker whispers in my ear and then kisses my cheek softly. I smile, and turn, wrapping my arms around him.

"I love it. Thank you." I whisper.

"That's not all," he whispers in my ear. "There's an even bigger not-so-surprise at the end of the night." He tells me. He grips my waist. I giggle.

"I look forward to it, Mr. West."

"K guys you can stop talking about your later plans and join the party," Leroy mutters while passing, laughing to himself. I laugh and let go of Parker. He just opts for my hand instead.

I take a sip of my wine and nod in appreciation at the taste.

Parker takes the wine from my hand and puts it down.

"I want you aware tonight. I want you to remember every detail. So no drinking. We can get smashed tomorrow, just not tonight."

"Or never." My brother pipes, walking by us to his wife and newborn child. I walk to them, my first time meeting the baby.

Me and Parker were at Disney while the child was being born. I had turned off my phone.

"What's his name?" I ask, smiling at the baby, who sports blonde hair and brown eyes. Uh oh. Future heartbreaker alert.

"Apollo Smith."

"He's beautiful," I say. Eileen, my brother's wife, hands him to me. I smile down at him and turn to Parker, whose eyes twinkle.

"Look. Isn't he adorable?"

"Yeah." He says, looking at me. I cradle the baby, who gurgles happily.

"I already love you, little Apollo. Awe he's so cute!" I squeal and give him back to Eileen, who smiles happily.

"Thank you. I know. We've created a beautiful child." Her eyes glint at my brother when she says that, and he smiles a true smile, and kisses her softly, playing with his son's hand.

It's a private moment, so I pull Parker away.

"I can't wait until that's us." He murmurs in my ear. I smile a true, full smile. I'm in this for the long run, so to hear that makes me happy.

"I love you," I whisper.

"And I love you."

He's about to kiss me when;

"Ahhhh hell nah, Pretty Parker, you have been hogging this girl all day as it is. Mm mm. It's my turn."

Ah, Hendrik.

"She's my girl, and I love her," Parker whines.

"I don't care," Hendrik says and snaps his fingers. "This bitch was mine way longer than she was yours honey bunny. I wanna get her all dolled up."

Hendrik grabs my wrist.

"Your gay-ness is showing strong," I comment with a smile. Hendrik laughs.

"All the time, sweetheart, all the time."

I wake up in a car.

Parker is driving, listening to Training Wheels by Melanie Martinez quietly.

Okay, but he's the only guy I know who listens to girls' music other than Hendrik and is still straight. It's... Weird. But nice. Because this song is sweet and it relates to us, how I call him fucking dumb for the stupid shit he does.

He pulls into a hotel parking lot. He looks over and smiles as he sees me fluttering my eyelashes at him.

"Hey, baby girl. Wake up, we're here."

"Where are we?"

"You don't remember?" He asks with an amused smile.

"No." I breathe and sit up. A sharp pain hits my head. I raise my hand to it and wince. He gets me medicine and a bottle of water.

"We're in Greenland."

"what." I hiss at him lowly.

"Yeah. We had that long ass plane flight. You were asleep most of it, so that makes sense but you were drunk the first hour and you kept whispering how you wanted to jump off of the plane and die. I'm jealous you don't remember."

"Oh," I mumble.

We get out and he grabs our bags. We go and check in before going to our room.

This is 5-star if I've ever seen it.

There's a goddamn hot tub for God's sake.

"My brother paid for this, didn't he?"

"Yup." He replies.

"Figures."

I give myself a tour and take note of how the bathtub is big enough for the both of us. I smile. I get undressed and put a bathrobe around me, keeping the top slightly open to show some cleavage.

I walk back to Parker to see him unpacking.

"Do you know where my black sweater is? I can't find... It..." He stops when he looks at me. His eyes trail down, a glazed look hitting his face as I lean on the doorway.

"I'm going to take a bath. Feel free to join if you'd like." I say, winking. He instantly walks towards the bathroom while taking his shirt off.

"I'm game."

I laugh and follow him in.

He gets undressed and gets in, sighing at the hot water.

"I get why girls do this now. I'm so doing this from now on." He sighs in ecstasy.

He looks at me and raises an eyebrow.

I slowly pull the string of the bathrobe and let it drop. He keeps his eyes on me, his breath hitching.

I get in and sit in between his legs, my back against his chest. He kisses my shoulder.

He grabs a washcloth and the liquid body soap that smells like roses. He smiles at me before putting the soapy cloth on my chest and cleaning me.

"Can't have you feeling icky, now, can we?" He whispers.

The way he pays such close attention to me, makes me feel this certain emotion I didn't feel much before at all. Ever.

"I feel... Special." I whisper, leaning my head back and kissing his jaw. "You make me feel special."

He smiles widely, a big, genuine, goofy grin.

"And you make me feel special as well. More than anyone else ever could." He tells me. I move closer to him. He groans. "I wouldn't do that if I were you."

"Why?"

"I think you know why."

So I move closer.

"So... What's the goal?" I ask him as we stare at a field of snow.

"To build an igloo. It's on the list." He tells me.

"And how the hell do we do that?" I ask him, confused.

"Just follow my lead."

After about two hours of soaked socks and gloves, the igloo is done. He goes into it slowly, and motions for me to come in. I do so.

It's dark and quiet, damp, and cold.

"We could fuck in here."

"Of course, you ruin the silence with something completely inappropriate. Classic Parker." I mutter. He smiles goofily, and I try to deny my own smile.

"You love it."

"I do."

"So is fucking in here off the table or..?"

"Parker."

"Yes?"

"Kindly shut the hell up."

"Okay. But, Ally?"

"Yes?"

"Women don't deserve rights."

And that's how I end up tackling him and slapping him, which makes the igloo collapse on us, and we can get our heads out, and slowly but surely get out, covered in snow, before making it back to the hotel, where instead of having round 2, I ignore him and go to bed.

But he still lies beside me and pulls me to him.

And I think that's what counts the most. Even though I'm slightly pissed at him, cold and tired and cranky, he doesn't get mad back or ignore me back, he just holds me.

And, this is why I love Parker West.

Chapter 24

It was two weeks later.

It was also currently Laney's birthday and she wanted the apartment for her and Sam, which was okay because Parker said he had something planned.

Ever since Parker's birthday, I seriously could just not stop getting enough of his skin, and every piece of him. We're what you'd call... Active. Very active.

But that's kind of private I guess.

I set my pencil down and stand up, handing in the paper first. People sigh. Someone asks me for answers, but I ignore them and go back to my seat.

People were still oddly confused about my and Parker's relationship and I couldn't understand why. We were just like any other couple.

Maybe except for the fact that I used to have depression. Speaking of, my cuts are completely healed and gone, so now my skin is flawless, other than my duck tramp stamp.

Suddenly, two people sit next to me.

I glance up at them from my book, confused.

"Are you and Parker still, like, a thing?" She asks.

"We've been dating for like 8 months... So yeah." I state awkwardly.

She pouts. "Oh. So.. Is he... You know... Good?"

"Good... At what?"

"Sex." She whispers.

"What I want to know is if you are." The guy suddenly whispers in my ear. I shrink away from them both, taking my cardigan and wrapping it around myself to cover my body.

"Um... That's none of your business."

"It's just a question." They both say.

"Get the hell away from her."

I sigh in relief.

I now notice that people have been watching us, and they look over at Parker in shock.

"Come on, baby. We gotta go."

I grab my bag and book.

"Where to?"

"It's a surprise, baby, come on." He smiles at me and holds out his hand. I take it. I hear sighs of want coming from some girls and some guy with them.

I smile and snuggle into his side.

"You're lucky I had already gotten my work done," I tell him.

"Mm, I know your work schedule like the back of my hand. You finish one paper within twenty minutes of having it. Plus there were only ten minutes of class left so I assumed you'd be done." He tells me. I hold his hand tightly.

He looks down at me. "Are you okay? What did they say to you?" He asks. I take in a breath and look away from him, about to open my mouth. "Don't lie, A."

I sigh. "She asked if you were good in bed... And then he... Said he wanted to know if I was... Good in bed that is."

He starts to turn around but I stop him.

"Don't, you'll lose your scholarship. It's not worth it." I tell him.

"Like hell, it isn't."

"Baby. Please." I step closer and run a hand under his shirt and trace his abs. He shivers slightly, and I fight a grin. "Let's go, you said you had a surprise?"

He smiles and kisses me before leading me to the parking lot. He has me get in the car, where I see two bags in the back. A cooler is back there and a tent.

"What..?"

"Shh." He smiles.

We drive to someone's house and they take the car and go in the directions Parker gives, and the guy tosses Parker's keys.

Parker gets on the motorcycle parked on the side of the road that has two helmets.

"Uh.. What?" I ask.

"Come on, Flower." He says with a smile. I hesitate. "Don't you trust me?"

I get on and put the helmet on without hesitation.

He smiles and puts on his helmet. He kicks it on and I jump in shock. He laughs.

"Hold on tight, baby!"

I hold on tight and shut my eyes.

He takes off, and I take a sharp breath. It's a feeling of freedom, adrenaline, and fright all at once. I clamp my arms tighter around him.

When he comes to a red light, he glances back at me.

"You good?" He asks.

"Yeah. It's fun. Kinda scary, but fun."

I see some girl in a car waving at me. I squint my eyes to see that chick from the plane on Parker's birthday.

I wave back, smiling slightly. I put my arm back on Parker just in time for him to go again.

After about an hour, we reach our destination; Lakeview Parks.

The guy with the car waits for us, and we swap vehicles again. I prefer the car if I'm being honest.

I notice the tent and fishing poles and cooler in the back.

"We're camping again?" I ask him.

"Yes, but this time we're fishing, not cliff diving. Unless you want to do that again." He informs me with a smile on his face.

"Sure."

He stops and gets us in before we find our camp spot.

It's very secluded and away from any other sites.

"You used my debit card, didn't you."

"Yeah."

"Figures."

He smiles. We get out and set up the tent in silence before getting our air very large sleeping bag in and our cooler. He puts our bags of clothes inside before getting the tackle box and fishing poles out of the car. I shut the door and lock it, and follow him to the river.

We go out onto the dock, and he gets everything set up.

He hands me my pole.

"How do I...?"

He smiles. "I love that you know nothing of all those 50 things. It makes me happy that you get to experience your first time for everything with me."

"Yeah yeah, show me how to use the damn thing," I demand. He laughs. I kiss him.

He puts his down and comes behind me.

His hands skim my arms on purpose before he gets to my hands. He shows me how to hold it, and I try not to be distracted that he's feeling me up practically.

He helps me cast it.

"Now we wait."

"Wait. Parker. Parker! It's tugging!"

He looks over and drops his pole on the deck.

I stand up quickly.

This must be a big ass fish because the pole is bending.

He grabs my hand and helps me pull.

After some time of pulling very hard, suddenly, a huge blue streak comes flying from the water and hits me in the face.

I drop the pole and stumble back, falling into the water as a result.

For a few seconds, I stay under and contemplate if life is really worth it, then I remember Parker is up there and decide it is.

I swim up and as soon as Parker sees me, all worry disappears, and he bursts into laughter. I crawl over and release the fish back into the water. I put the pipe down and stare at Parker laughing, tears coming from his eyes, a broad smile on his features, looking so damn cute and happy.

So I smile, looking at him. He makes me happy. Very, very happy. Special. Loved. Wanted. Needed. Cared for. Adored. He makes me feel like myself and sees us as we are.

He finally stops and looks at me.

"What are you looking at? Is there broccoli in my teeth?"

"You don't eat broccoli."

"Oh right."

I step closer and wrap my arms around him. He wrinkles his nose but hugs me back.

Just before I pull away from the hug, I push him into the water.

And this time, it was my turn to laugh.

This tent Parker had bought has a see-through roof thing. Don't understand it but basically, we can see the stars and moon.

Our hair was wet from showering at the park showers, and we both smelt like Parker's body wash.

He pulls me closer to him.

"As much as I would love to make love tonight, I think it's a cuddle kind of night," Parker tells me. I nod in agreement. I wrap my arm around his waist and put one leg in between his legs. He kisses my forehead softly.

"I love you so much." He whispers.

"And I love you so much. More than you could ever imagine."

"Mm, I bet I can imagine. I bet we love each other equally." He says. "Nah, I love you more."

"No way. I love you more."

"No, I love yooouuu more!"

It went on like that for much longer.

Looking back on it, it was a stupid game with one result. One of us loved each other more.

I guess I won the game of "I love you more."

Chapter 25

I wake to Parker shaking me urgently. My eyes snap open.

"What? What?!" I ask quickly. "Are you okay?! Is it Jordan?"

I notice it's dark out, but just a tiny tiny tint of light out.

"Let's go watch the sunrise. It's on the list, and then we can watch it set tonight." He tells me. I let out a breath.

"Don't scare me like that, Parker!" I snap at him.

"Shhh. Come on, baby girl." He says, taking my hand and forcing me to follow him out. My heart melts.

I have been feeling anxious lately.

I know that we already talked about what would happen when the list was over, but there were only 10 things left, one of which we were about to do, so 9.

I love him. A lot.

I'm scared that he's going to leave.

I squeeze his hand tighter. He smiles at me, and I give a weak one in return.

I can see it on his face that he can tell something is bothering me, but he doesn't say anything for now.

We go to the deck and sit down. I take my flip-flops off and dip my feet in the water, lying my head on his shoulder and watching across the water. The sky slowly and gradually is turning lighter.

"What's wrong, Ally? For the past few days, you keep thinking about something at random times. Tell me what's on your mind, Princess."

I inwardly sigh at his words.

"I-I know we talked about this but... The list is almost done." I whisper. He laughs quietly.

"I don't get why that stresses you so much. You should be glad it's almost over. That'll mean you've done all those things." He says.

"I noticed a fault in the list. One of the numbers said, 'Let go of my past'. I realized that Melinda never did let go of her past." I tell him. "I just... I don't know. The only reason we ever spoke was because of the list."

"No, it was not, Ally." He laughs loudly.

"What do you mean?"

"Okay. Let me tell you my side of the story. So my friend Ty and I walk into Starbucks after class. Our other friend was waiting for us at a table. We start walking there, and I do a scan of the room. My eyes land on the most beautiful thing I've ever seen: Allison Smith. Everyone knew her, obviously. She was so gorgeous that you couldn't not know her. She didn't even notice the attention she had. Guys talked about wanting to get with her, girls talked about wanting to look like her. I've heard it all. She was wearing a grey sweater, blue skinny jeans, and black boots, and was typing at a computer and sipping her drink. I was so distracted that my friend pushed me over to her, but I fell on the chair like an idiot. Your bag fell. I picked up the papers with you and saw the list. I scanned it really quickly and was surprised at it. But I didn't care about it either. I found it amusing almost but not sad at all. Cool. That one day you could do all these things with someone. And that's when you looked into my eyes for the first time. That's why I was so shocked, Ally. Not because you never went out like you said a few weeks ago, but because your eyes are my favorite color. Aqua blue. It was love at first sight, I just didn't know it."

He tells me. Tears build in my eyes.

Then he says something that completely and utterly shocks me to the core.

"The list was just an excuse to talk to you because I didn't have the guts. Especially not when it came to someone so perfect. And I fell in love. And you fell back. And we caught each other and we're going to have the best life together imaginable. I can't wait to marry you, buy a house with you, have kids with you, and grow old with you. That's my list, Ally. Those 4 things. It will happen to us. I know it because you are meant for me 100%."

Tears fall from my eyes. I kiss him while laughing slightly, happier than I ever have been.

He kisses me back, softly, smiling into the kiss. He pulls away first and hands me a pair of sunglasses. We both put a pair on and then watch.

The sun suddenly peaks through the ground. Slowly, over about the course of half an hour, it rises.

I sigh, happy, and content.

In a little bit, it started to rain.

Parker looks at me from across the tent and smiles devilishly. "Number 47!" He says.

He grabs my hand and drags me out.

He sets his hands on my waist after taking my hands and putting them around his neck.

I stare into his honey eyes.

"There's no music," I whisper.

"We don't need it." He tells me, before placing a soft kiss on my lips. We begin to sway slowly. And at one point he dips me and winks at me before kissing me again.

I rest my head against his chest and listen to his heartbeat. The beat is fast. It's the most beautiful sound I've ever heard, better than the music we didn't need.

"Do you hear that? How fast you make my heart race?" He asks me. My heart melts. I begin to cry. He looks at me. "Why are you crying?" He asks.

"I just love you so much." I babble. He smiles again.

"And I love you, always."

We watched the sunset.

8 things left on the list.

But I'm not scared anymore. Because I love Parker, and I know that he loves me.

We'll go to school. We'll come home and take care of Jordan.

We've been talking about moving in with each other. Since Laney is moving into Sam's apartment, he's going to move in with me, and I couldn't be happier because the thought of waking up every morning to his face is delightful.

Now, going home, a comfortable silence around Parker and me as he drives with one hand and has the other intertwined with mine, I feel calm and happy.

I feel at peace. With myself. With everything. It felt like there was never anything wrong with me or my past. I never had an addiction, my parents were out of my mind, and my best friend never killed herself. That's what it felt like.

But it wasn't reality.

And as a cruel reminder decided to come my way, that was when the other car slammed into ours.

Everything felt hazy.

Like I was having a really good dream.

White. Everything was white. It was a blank canvas of nothing at first.

Then, colors slowly began to fill in around me.

Green grass. Trees were all around the small meadow, where flowers were.

Two women sat in the meadow, facing away from me. I blink a few times and slowly stumble forward.

I'm in a white dress. My hair is around me in beautiful waves.

I approach slowly. They turn.

I halt.

"Ally, come join us. We're having tea and biscuits, your favorite." Melinda smiles warmly at me.

"No... No this isn't real. This isn't real. Where am I? Who are you?" I ask, my heart hurting.

Melinda and my mother sit there, smiling at me.

"Honey, don't be ridiculous. You know who we are." My mother says. "It's so nice to finally see you again. You were such a beautiful baby. I just wish this wasn't so soon. You're beautiful."

"Where am I?" I ask weakly.

"You're in the middle. You're in between life and death. We came to talk. To convince you."

I walk forward and sit with them. I take a glass of tea.

"Convince me to...?"

"Live," Melinda says.

"Why? If I'm going to die, why not now?" I ask bitterly.

"Many reasons. You're young and beautiful. The note I gave you months ago which you haven't read yet," Melinda glares slightly, "there's something important in there to be read. Your friends who care about you and are crying in the hallway right now. And your boyfriend who is completely frozen and crying by himself in the hall as they continue to pump your heart. There's still hope."

"But.. I... I missed you. I always wanted to know you. I want to stay."

"You can't, sweetheart." My mom says. "I died so you could live. Please. Don't make that all for nothing. Don't take everything you have for granted. Your brother is sitting out there thinking he's about to lose one of the best things to ever happen to him."

Tears well in my eyes.

"You have to make a choice," Melinda says. "Please, don't make the wrong one."

I take a deep breath and think.

"Sis, I love you and all, but you're a mess."

"Shut up, it's not like you're any better!" I laugh in glee.

"Honey, you are rockin' that dress. Parker is going to fah-lip when he sees you." Hendrik says with a smile.

"Ally, you should get out more often." Laney smiles at me.

"Do you hear that? How fast you make my heart race?"

"I'm a selfish, a very very selfish man. You're mine, okay?"

"Give me a second, you just keep taking my breath away."

"I love you."

And that's the moment I decided I would live.

I woke up seconds later after the doctors were all sighing in relief from my heart beating again.

They fired questions at me and ran tests in the room, to find out that I was perfectly okay other than the broken ribs and hand I have.

I asked them if they'd told everyone I was okay, and they said no, so I told them to let them in.

They have me lie down fully, gently easing me.

Everything is hazy, a different hazy than the dream thing where I was in the middle or whatever.

Parker barges in first and sighs in relief when I meet his eyes. I smile weakly at him. He comes to my side instantly and takes my good hands and kisses my knuckles softly, still crying.

I made the right choice.

"I was so scared." He whispers. "Don't ever scare me like that again. I love you. I love you so, so much." He says, his shoulders shaking with silent sobs.

"I love you too, Parker. I love you too." I tell him. I fix his hair, and he smiles lightly at me.

"Ally." My brother says in relief when he enters the room. I smile at him.

"Hey, brother."

We all catch up. I was out for two days. I have to stay here for a week. I asked Laney to bring me the note addressed to me in the second drawer of my bedside table. She did so.

That night, after I forced Parker to go home, alone in the hospital room, I opened the letter.

Ally,

This is the most unfair thing for me to ever do. I get that.

When you receive this letter, it will have been two years since I've died. When you finally read this, call the number at the bottom and get everything sorted out. I have a lot to say.

I was in a bad place. Too bad for my own good. And if I know you, you still blame yourself for a choice I consciously made on my own. It isn't your fault. It's mine.

When he cheated on me, it hurt me too much. And I may sound weak and pathetic but I couldn't give a damn because that's the truth. I thought he was the one for me. And that cut too deep. I couldn't take it. That's why I ended my life.

Now the other thing I have to tell you.

I have a child. If you recall, a week before I passed away I had come home from a mental hospital in which I was there to 'get better'. That was a lie and coverup. I was pregnant during those six months of being away. I gave birth to my child there. For now, my mother has custody.

Ally, she isn't the godmother. She isn't supposed to have my child.

You are the godmother. It's on the legal papers and I specifically requested in my will for you to take the child if you wanted when you read this letter and called the number, which is my lawyer.

I know that this is a lot to put on you. It's all your choice whether or not you'd like to take care of my child. I'd never blame you if you didn't.

I love you, Ally. You are my best friend. Forever. You gave me hope that even in dark situations, you could come out on top. But I am not strong enough for that. But you are.

I'll see you on the other side, hopefully when you're old and grey.

Be there or be a loser,

Infinitely yours,

Melinda.

#***-****

I pick up my phone and dial the number.

"Hello, Kyro Law, Mr. Davenport speaking."

"Hi. My name is Allison Smith, and I'm calling for the custody of Melinda Hawthorne's child."

Chapter 26

It was finally summer vacation.

Parker surprised me this morning with a very nice present.

"Parker," I whine. "Come on, what is it already?" I ask him, irritated.

"Hold on!" He says.

"You seriously stopped in the middle of sex for whatever this is? Come on, Parker, please just find it later. I need you right now." I complain.

"Hold on, woman!" He screams at me. "This is why you guys shouldn't have rights because all you do is nag and n-"

"When I'm about to hit euphoria because of your body, Parker, and you stop to find something in your bag, yeah I'm gonna be mad!" I yell back at him.

I'm glad Laney isn't home.

"Oh yeah? You really liked what I was doing there with the Oh I found it!" He says.

He's a sight. A stark naked Adonis bringing me an envelope.

He hands it to me with a smile. I bring the blanket up to cover myself but he tugs it back down.

"I like looking at you," he says, smiling. My heartbeat picks up.

I open it to see two tickets to Hawaii.

"Holy shit, Parker!" I gasp in shock. "You got these for us?" I ask him.

"Yeah. We're going to stay in this really awesome house by the beach for three nights, and in front of the bed there's a glass sliding door so we can stare at the ocean but if we want privacy there's blinds." He tells me. I put them on my bedside table before kissing him roughly.

And we pick up where we left off.

It was a day later, and after being teased about the whole mortal combat thing at practice (the basketball matches are still ongoing, until the last match which is in a few weeks, I am tired.

Parker and I got back to my place and I realized that I wasn't in a good mood today.

Parker is in a good mood- men and their after-effects of sex- but I just wasn't.

I wasn't feeling happy or confident today.

I went into the bathroom without a word. Parker looked confused. I look at myself in the mirror and frown.

There is just something about me that I don't like.

Maybe it's my slightly pointy nose. Or how my hair is mad frizzy. Or how awkward I look.

I glance down at my legs. Parker loves my legs but I don't. My old scars are still slightly visible if you look hard enough.

I look back in the mirror and inspect my eyes. I remember a time when they would be red from either being high or crying, always one or the other.

My arms seem to be slightly chubby.

God, I hate myself.

Do I always look this bad? Did I gain weight? Am I ugly? Why do I look so repulsive?

Tears build in my eyes.

I put my hands against the sink and lowered my head, a tear dripping.

Will Parker leave me if I get fat? Or if I become even uglier?

"Baby, what's wrong?" Parker asks softly from behind me. I jump slightly in shock that he's there, but don't move. "Why were you looking at yourself in the mirror like that? What are you thinking? What's wrong?"

"Why are you with me?" I ask him. I look up, looking at him through the mirror. His eyes widen in shock upon my tear-stained face.

"What do you mean?" He whispers, questioning with a nervous edge to his tone.

"Look at me. I'm an ex-drug addict, I'm fucking ugly, I swear it's not me, I'm getting fat, okay? I'm just... There's nothing good about me." I explain to him. His face breaks.

"Why would you think that? I thought you were getting better with this. I thought I was helping you." He murmurs.

"Helping me with what?"

"Your insecurities." He tells me. "You're fucking beautiful is what you are, Ally. I love your little pointy nose, those perfect plump lips, and your long black hair, I love the way your body curves perfectly and fits against mine like a puzzle piece. I love your long and beautiful legs, those faint old scars remind me that you stopped hurting yourself because I came into your life, and that makes me happy, and you make me happy because you're so incredible and sweet, kind, funny, loving, caring, beautiful, and I just love you so much."

"Why are you lying to me?" I ask, sobbing. "Stop lying!"

"I'm not, princess! You're perfect. Perfect." He says, leading me out of the bathroom and onto my living room couch. He sits down and pulls me to his side. I cry into his shoulder, weakly putting my arms around his waist.

I whimper, pain and sadness filling me. I don't even know what's taken over me. I haven't gotten like this in many months.

"Baby, what happened? You were okay earlier, what happened?" He asks softly, stroking my hair.

"I-I don't know. I just got really really sad." I whisper, tears still falling. He wipes them away.

"How about we watch some movies, eat whatever you want, drink whatever you want, cuddle and I can shower you in kisses and not be able to, but try, to explain just how much I love you?" He offers. I smile slightly, sniffing. "There's that pretty smile I love so much. Open your eyes, I want to see you." He coaxes.

I do as he says and open my eyes.

He smiles.

"There you are. Hi, love." He coos. I giggle, snuggling into his side. He smiles and wraps his arms around me.

"Thank you," I whisper.

"Ally, I need to ask you a very serious question," Parker states. I nod. "Do you still have depression?"

I freeze. "Ally." He says.

When I don't respond, he sits me up. Pain shows on his face. I swallow and look at my lap, fiddling with my hands.

"Will you please answer my question?"

"Second drawer, bedside table," I tell him. He stands and goes into my room.

"What the hell, Ally?!" He yells, exasperated. I take a shaky breath when he comes back with my prescription and the gun I have considered using several times. "What the fuck." He demands. "What kind of sick shit is this?! Why would you hide this from me?" He asks loudly.

I shake my head, tears falling again.

"God, I never knew it was possible to love, hate, be mad, and despair for someone at once." He says. I shut my eyes and covered my face. I clutch my hair and pull it.

I let out a shuddered breath.

"Why?" He asks. "Why? What is this for?" He asks, lightly lifting the gun.

"I used to think about death a lot. Every day. It stopped when you came into my life, but, lately over the past month.." I whisper. I look away, hiding my face.

"What's the two boxes in there?" He asks. I tell him to go get them for me and he places them on my lap.

Two wooden boxes. I trace the M on the first one and open it. I trace the A on the second one and open it.

The first item in the boxes: was the friendship bracelet we both had.

Second item: the pair of panties she wore for her first item, and in my box, the pair I had worn for my first time.

Third item: the first lipstick we had ever owned.

It continues.

These boxes hold mine and Melinda's first things.

"It's something she put together for herself when she..." I blow a breath out. "Her mom gave it to me to solve. It symbolized all her firsts. I decided to do the same for when I.."

"Ally," Parker says in a broken tone.

"After we had started dating, I stopped putting things in there. But then we made love for the first time and it was just this subconscious thing and I put them in there and before I knew it... My box matched hers. All except one item, which I can't tell you about." I tell him.

"Ally. You have hidden enough from me. What is the item?"

"It's.. A photo of Melinda's daughter."

He takes a shocked breath.

"Why did you keep all of this, especially the gun?" He asks. I sigh.

"...I don't know," I whisper. My bottom lip starts to tremble. "I don't know." I sob out again. I shut the boxes quickly.

Parker pulls me to him.

He waits for me to calm down, stroking my back, and I feel a hot tear fall on my shoulder. I hold him tighter.

"I'm sorry." I apologize quickly. "I'm so sorry. I should have told you, explained to you how I was feeling, and shouldn't have hidden anything from you." I tell him.

"It's alright, baby, it's okay." He whispers soothingly in my ear.

"Parker?" I ask.

"Could you do me a favor?"

"What is it? Anything, I promise."

"I need a distraction. Make love to me?" I ask softly.

He doesn't waste time in helping me escape from my own mind.

This is why I love Parker West so much.

I grip onto Parker's arm. He smiled at me, from what I could see in the mask we were both wearing.

We're in a large cage together, and it's being lowered into the ocean off of the banks of Hawaii.

Then we are under. It goes lower for a while longer then stops. We have gear covering us so we can breathe.

Everything is quiet. Fish start swimming all around us. A shark passes by. Another shark.

We can see a coral reef, all the plants, fish, and everything underwater life. My eyes well up. It's beautiful.

I feel Parker's hand in mine.

I feel happy.

Suddenly a mass from the side comes straight at us. I scream as the shark bangs its head on the cage, trying to open it to eat us. Parker pulls the rope that alerts them that we want to be pulled up.

After a few minutes, we're finally off.

"Never doing that again," I state, taking off the gear and giving it to the instructor, who laughs easily. Parker nods in agreement.

We wave goodbye and move on. We go to the beach bar, where the girls there give me and Parker both Hawaiian outfits to wear and push us to the dressing room.

They gave me one of their dancing skirts and a floral bra/crop top thing. I get a pair of my white high-heeled wedges and put the ensemble on.

When I step out, Parker's gaze rakes my body.

"As much as I love it, I can't allow men to look at what's mine." He tells me. The girl dancers giggle at him and drag me from him, and sit me down on a chair. He follows but they make him stay back.

They're doing my hair with flowers in it and putting little clips and glitter in my hair like them. They do my makeup to match my bra and flower color - figure it's Aqua blue.

They finally turned me around.

Parker smiles at me a little.

"Beautiful! Come dance with us!" A girl says. They don't really give me a choice seeing as they take me over to a clearing and start instructing me on how to do their dance.

I blush while doing it.

"You're really good! A natural!" Someone tells me.

A guy whistles while looking me up and down. Parker glares at him quickly.

Finally, I get the dance down.

I mean, this is mad awkward, belly dancing with a bunch of strangers in front of strangers cheering us on and my boyfriend recording me.

When the dance ends, applause rises, and they give me one of those flower necklaces.

I'm given all of the girls' numbers, and their boss tells me that if I ever want a job that gives me a place to stay with it, she's the one to come to. I thank her, and she gives me her number as well.

Parker smiles at me when I return to him, and shows me his newest Instagram post, which is of me dancing with those girls.

"For someone who doesn't like people seeing what is his, he sure likes to post it," I say. He smiles wider.

"I just like to show off what's mine, if I'm honest, baby." He says, and I blush at the nickname. "People are commenting on things I don't like, though."

I take his phone and read the comments.

I could just cum to this

She's so hot

Damn

Man u lucky asf

Want any one of those girl's numbers, especially the blue ones.

I cringe and give him it back.

"That's your fault for being popular," I state. His jaw drops.

"Because thousands of people watch college basketball and follow me? That's a little unfair." He says. I shrug. He smiles and kisses my forehead. I shut my eyes while his lips longer there, smiling, and I hear the click of his camera.

"Let's go get dinner, we have reservations at their really nice place by the beachside." He tells me. I take his hand and lead us over.

It's around 7 PM, but the sun is still up. We get in quickly, perfect timing for our dinner, and sit down at a table by a window. He takes my hand across the table.

We eat dinner, in bliss, me feeling relaxed and in a good mood.

When we get the bill, we tense up.

"Why the fuck is lobster so expensive, you guys have a million here!?" He hisses more to himself.

"Parker... I have an idea." I tell him. "The list, become fake engaged to get free food! Let's try it!" I tell him. He smiles and nods.

He stands and makes his way over to me, before getting on one knee. I cover my mouth in shock and gasp loudly. People look over, and everyone starts staring.

"I know that right now I don't have the ring because I'm an idiot like you always tell me, and I forgot it at home on my bed, but, Allison Smith, I want to spend my entire future with you. I love you, not to the moon and back, but to Neptune and back. Hell, even Pluto and that's not even a planet anymore. You're it for me. I know it. So say I'm it for you too, and marry me." He asks.

People are recording.

"Yes! Yes, of course, I'll marry you, you idiot!" I exclaim. He pulls me into his arms and swings me around, and kisses me passionately. I put my arms around his neck and kissed him back.

Applaud erupts.

As expected, we got dinner free, and each of us got a free slice of cake. On our cakes, are mood rings that they sell at the souvenir shop. We both put them on. We eat the cake, thank the staff, and leave. After we're gone, we laugh to ourselves.

We get back to our little beachside hut, where all our bags wait, and sigh, staring at each other.

"We've talked about everything. We know each other through and through. Name something to do now, baby," Parker says. I give him a pointer finger and go to the bathroom.

One of my bags was waiting there. I shut the door and changed into the aqua-blue lingerie set, that has this little see-through shawl. It's just so cute.

I take the flowers out and shake what I can shake out of the glitter.

I step out to see the lights dimmed, rose petals on the bed, and candles lit. Parker holds out a glass of champagne. I take it while smiling.

"You don't cease to amaze me," I tell him. Tears build in my eyes.

"Why are you crying?" He asks instantly.

"...You make me feel so loved," I whisper. "So cared for. I love you so, so much." I tell him. He smiles.

"And I love you." He murmurs, caressing the side of my face with his free hand. I lean into his warm touch and let my eyes shutter closed. His thumb traces my bottom lip. "You make me feel special." He admits. "Like someone actually cares enough to listen to how I feel, what I want, where I see myself in the future."

"Where is that?" I whisper, distracted slightly by his touch.

"Right next to you." He tells me. We both decide to quickly drink our champagne and set the glasses down. Parker pushes me gently to the bed. I lay down and smile at him from where he stands, leaning over me.

"Ally, Ally, Ally." He murmurs.

"Yes?" I whisper.

"I'm gonna make you feel how worshipped you are."

Chapter 27

"Finally." Parker groans as he drops his bags in our apartment. Parker has officially moved in as of right before we left for vacation. I miss Laney, but she still calls every day to check up on me.

"I have a deal for you," I tell Parker.

"Does it involve what I asked earlier?" He asks. I nod once. "Okay, what is it?"

"If you watch all the Twilight movies with me, I'll suck your dick," I tell him. He thinks for a long few seconds.

"No thank you, not worth it." He shakes his head. "When does Jordan come home?" He asks me.

"I'll pick him up when I come home from an errand I have to run tomorrow," I tell him.

"Errand?" He asks, and I follow him to the kitchen where he gets a glass of whIskey for us both.

"Yes. Errand." I reply, not letting him know.

I'm going to finally be able to visit my godchild tomorrow. I finally get to meet her. I wonder if she looks like him or her.

Does she have her father's black hair or Melinda's perfect blonde locks? His brown eyes, or her blue ones? His personality, or hers?

"Where are you going?" He asks me.

"Out." I laugh. He shoots me a look.

"What are you hiding from me?" He asks in a curt tone. I just look at him. "Ally. Is it something important?" He asks. I give in, and nod. He takes my face in his hands. "How long have you been hiding whatever this is from me?" He asks.

"Since we got in that car crash," I whisper.

"Ally, what the fuck." He says in a blank tone, tearing himself away from me. "What the hell are you hiding?"

"I just don't know how to tell you," I admit.

"Just spit it out."

"I have a goddaughter, Parker, and it's in the will that I eventually gain custody of her and I don't know what to do." I let him know.

He gapes at me.

"Wait... So... We basically have a kid..?" He asks.

"We?" I ask.

"Ally, I'm in this for the long run. What's yours is mine and what's mine is yours." He tells me. I reach over and press my lips to his. He kisses back softly, drawing me into his hold, which causes my knees to go weak. He makes me all jelly-like.

His hands wander along my body, like an interested tourer along a treasure map.

He lifts me and places me on the counter, standing between my legs.

"Did you say that just to get laid?" I ask him, smiling. He shakes his head. "Too bad, 'cause it would have worked."

My breath shakes, I'm nervous. Parker grips my hand tightly. I ring the doorbell.

After a minute of shuffling, the door opens. Melinda's mother stands there with a smile, which widens upon seeing me.

"Ally! Oh, it's been so long! I've missed you spending the nights and helping me with dinner while Mel was all lazy." She laughs quietly. I smile weakly and nod.

"I've missed you too, Mrs. Hawthorne," I tell her, hugging her. Once she releases me, Parker takes my hand again. "This is my boyfriend, Parker," I tell her. He introduces himself better quickly.

She leads us in.

"Mia is playing right now, come on. I'll introduce you formally as her godmother." She tells me with a smile.

My heart skips a beat. We follow her to a pink door.

"She's quite obsessed with anything Disney princess." She laughs. She opens the door.

In the room, is a little girl with blonde hair, exactly like her mother's. Tears build in my eyes. She should be around 4 years old. The little girl looks up, revealing caramel-colored eyes.

She almost looks like Parker, with her hair coloring and eye color, but her father had the same eye color and those are definitely Melinda's locks.

She smiles.

"Hi! I'm Mia!" She says, coming forward and shaking my hand. "Gramma told me someone was coming to visit. I didn't know it was two people!" She says. I fall to my knees in front of her and pull her in my arms. She makes a confused "huh?" But hugs me back.

"Mia, this is your mother's best friend, and your godmother, Allison." Mrs. Hawthorne tells her.

"God mother?" Mia asks.

"It means that before your mother passed away, she made it to where Allison would take care of you. Live at her home, she would feed you and such."

"Where have you been then, Godmother?" Mia asks me. I smile slightly as she wipes my tears off my cheeks.

"I didn't know until recently. But I'm here now, okay? That's all that matters." I whisper.

"Can I call you mum then, if you're my Godmother?" She asks.

"I-if you want," I tell her.

"Okay, mom." She says. More tears spring to my eyes. "Come here, we were just having a tea party with Belle and Cinderella, and you, boy, " she says to Parker, "go fetch us some cookies." She says, her head raised slightly. Something about her definitely demands attention and gives her the power instantly.

"Just like her mom." I laugh quietly.

"What was she like?" She asks me. A deep sorrow fills me because I've asked that same question to my brother.

"She was powerful. Everyone at school loved her, and she was the most popular girl. I didn't have many friends because

I wasn't pretty, and I was shy and quiet, but your mother was so amazing, that she decided to make friends with the loner. She was kind, beautiful -just like you- and she was just... Incredible. To be in her presence was to give your attention to her completely. It just worked that way. You have her mouth, her nose, and her perfect princess-like hair."

Parker and Mrs. Hawthorne come back with the cookies.

"I wish I could have met her." She says wistfully.

"I wish you could have too," I tell her.

"Did you know your mother?" She asks me.

"No, she passed away while giving birth to me," I explain to her. She smiles a tiny bit.

"I'm sorry. At least we know how each other feels." She says. Damn, this girl is mature and intelligent as fuck.

"Cheers to that."

Parker looks over at me, smiling.

"Why are we here?" I ask him. It's now nighttime, and we left the Hawthorne's. We went out to a 24-hour diner and ate and talked until midnight, and are now in front of a park.

"Let's do something crazy." He says. "Let's take off our clothes, go streaking in the park, and then hop into the water over there. There are no lights and no one around. It's on the list." He says.

I bite my lip, considering, before taking off my shirt. We break into laughter while taking all our clothes off. He turns all the car lights off before we get out. The wind is slightly chilly against my bare skin, and I feel nervous.

He walks over to me and takes my hand. I kiss him before taking off, laughing loudly when I look back and see his shocked expression.

He runs after me quickly and is catching up quickly.

Suddenly a hard feeling hits my stomach. I tumble over the park bench, instantly groaning.

Parker is almost screaming with the way he's laughing so loudly. He helps me up. I shove him into the water quickly, and he yelps.

"Not cool, dude!" He complains and splashes water at me. I jump in quickly, laughing.

We swim around for a bit, holding onto each other, kissing softly, and laughing freely.

Suddenly, two flashlight beams are on us.

"You're under arrest."

Chapter 28

Three seconds can make a huge difference.

1. Parker's form went back to normal, and he threw the ball.

The girl finally came to stand beside me. I turn to her, life in slow motion.

2. "I fu-"

The ball made it in. Cheers erupted, but my ears were on what this girl had just told me.

"What?" I ask her quietly. People have Parker on their shoulders. They start to make their way to me. The girl grabs my wrist and tugs me away before everyone else can.

Parker stares at me with confusion.

She led me down a hall, it was silent.

"What do you mean by you fucked my boyfriend?" I ask her, my voice shaking.

"Last weekend. At that party, you said he could go to. We were both drunk, and.."

My ears rang. I stepped back from her.

"Ally, I'm really sorry," she whispers, but I can see her trying not to smirk, the satisfaction in her eyes at seeing me break.

I walk. Then I run.

There's no way.

No.

Why would he do this?

Why wouldn't he tell me?

Why would he lie?

How long has he been lying?

Did Parker West ever even love me? Or did he just want me because number 10 on the list is sex? Was this all a plan to fuck me?

But then why did he stay so long?

When you break trust, you have nothing to show for yourself.

Was what this girl saying to me true?

Epilogue

I pretended, for now, that I didn't hear a thing she said. I wouldn't let Parker think something was wrong. Not yet.

After a while, and a celebratory dinner, we finally got home.

"Are you okay? You've been quiet ever since that girl pulled you into the hall." He states, his eyebrows drawn together.

"Yeah... Yeah, I'm fine."

"Ally, don't lie to me. What's wrong?"

I stared at him, not knowing what to say. I didn't even realize that tears were slipping when they were.

He pulled me into his arms and held on tightly. I didn't want to believe that he could do this, to me, to us.

He pulls me into our room.

I don't know why I did it, but I begged him to distract me.

The fucked up part about it? He could have slept with another woman (well I don't know for sure yet) and I just turned around and slept with him again.

Why?

It took me a few minutes to understand.

Because I knew, I knew it was true. And I knew that I would be leaving.

"Ally? Are you asleep?" He asks. I give labored breathing and pretend I'm sleeping. "I'm sorry. I was drunk, I didn't mean to. Maybe I'll admit this to your face, awake, soon. There's more to the story, a hell of a lot more-"

I stopped listening after the "didn't mean to" part.

He just confirmed it.

I waited until he fell asleep. I stood and looked at his form, sleeping, peaceful. He's so physically perfect. No one should have the right to look like th- snap out of it, he cheated on you!

Leave. Go. Run, run from this. Like you always do. You're weak, might as well let it be known now. Go, Ally.

I grabbed his shirt, undergarments, and some joggers and pulled them on. I get shoes on. I quietly get a suitcase and rummage for my stuff. I get clothes, shoes, and most impor-tantly, my gun. I stuff it all in there rapidly.

I leave around 2 in the morning, my heart heavy with grief, and crying.

Such a bittersweet ending, Parker and I's love story.

As I drove, further and further away from him, the slower my tears came, and the colder my heart felt.

That was the last time I'd ever see Parker West, sleeping, just admitting his sin, thinking about how perfect he was, and how much I loved him, no matter how much I wished I didn't.

Not.

I would see him again.

After all, the list hasn't been completed.